WITH
TIES THAT
BIND

WITH TIES THAT BIND

Broken Bonds, Book Two

TRISHA WOLFE

Interior Design and Formatting by:

www.emtippettsbookdesigns.com

There is always some madness in love. But there is also always some reason in madness.

~Friedrich Nietzsche

CHAPTER 1

COLD FISH

ALPHA

*T*here's a misunderstanding in modern culture, that of the psychopath. I blame writers. Hollywood scriptwriters, novelists. They're lethargic. Want a villain? Make him a psychopathic serial killer!

No motive. No history, really. Just a means to an end for your lazy plot.

The truth, on the contrary, is typically and usually not as entertaining.

Let's take statistics, shall we? One-percent of the population are high-functioning psychopaths. This is a fact. They're not serial killers chasing you with a giant kitchen knife, covered in blood, laughing manically... They're your neighbors, your family, your doctors and your lawyers. They're the people in authority; the people who you trust.

And you need them.

You need them to be callous and unfeeling when it comes to the tough decisions. You need them to be a cold fish. Wars are not won with empathy. Cities and kingdoms were not built with your indecisive sympathies. Compassion does not prosper.

I take a long drag from my cigarette and sigh out a plume of smoke. I watch the tendrils waft upward, out and over the carnage, as I roll the white filter between my finger and thumb. It's stained red, matching the dark crimson blanketing the cement.

I loathe stereotypes. So the irony that I've now lowered myself to the stereotypical psychopath, for me, is deplorable. I spit on filth like Wells and Mason—men who have no impulse control. I'm above them in every way, and yet here I am, covered in blood after committing a very impulsive act.

"Clean this mess," I order Donavan, my right-hand man. Having taken Alex's spot, he hops to, anxious to prove his worth. For now, he's a good little henchman. Much like Alex King used to be.

An internal ache pangs somewhere beneath my breastbone, the loss of Alex still fresh. It was a necessary sacrifice, but still, I don't savor the ultimate cost in lowering my ranks. It's hard to find good, dedicated men. Men who will serve without question. Who will devote their very lives to the job.

In truth, Alex didn't have to die. I could've salvaged him. Could've scolded him in some public fashion, and no one would've thought less of me. He was my favorite, after all.

Groomed and mentored by myself, and the men all looked up to him.

And that, my friends, is why he had to be made an example of.

Not because of his faults or the one mistake that cost me the medical examiner. He had to be taken out because there cannot be dissension in the ranks.

It was the perfect opportunity to disgrace him and reinforce my authority, to which there should never be any question.

King Henry said it best: *Uneasy lies the head that wears a crown.* Ah, Shakespeare. The fundament of knowledge. Whenever in doubt, I can always turn to him for guidance.

It's lonely at the top.

But the second it's not, the second I feel there's another soul I can lay my burdens on…that's the moment I'll feel a knife in my back.

I kneel beside my once busty blonde and tilt my head. Let my gaze drag over her unseeing eyes, still features. Breathless. Timeless. A moment captured and suspended, immortalizing her, and her torment. She'll never look as beautiful as she does this very second. Her skin still warm, blushing her cheeks. Glassy eyes widened in an almost awe-like expression.

With a gloved hand, I brush aside the wayward tresses clinging to her lip-gloss. "You have a purpose now, sweetness."

From the neck down, it's difficult to distinguish what's flesh and what's bone—what's woman left of her mutilated

3

carcass. The brand my girls don on their thighs was removed with the first flaying. Her lovely, full breasts skinned from her body.

"Wrap her up and deliver the package," I command.

As I stand, I peer over the sea of dead girls littering the floor. Such a waste, such a shame. And I, the cold fish, swimming in this sea of red. I'm stained by it. It's how my kingdom was forged, how I now wear my heavy crown, but it's tainted the very earth I stand upon.

I flick the butt away and step over the blonde. There's a small niggle of remorse in the pit of my stomach, but it's easily snuffed out. Like the cherry of my cigarette as it sizzles out in a pool of blood.

CHAPTER 2

ARMAGEDDON

QUINN

*T*he shouting is an irritating background noise to my chaotic thoughts as they become increasingly and impatiently louder. Captain Wexler is giving me his signature ass-chewing. One I've earned and would feel badly about if it wasn't for the imploding case I need to get back to.

"Are you hearing me, Quinn?"

Snapped out of my daze, I shift my gaze from Avery loitering in the bullpen on the other side of the glass wall to Wexler's inflamed face. "I am, sir." The annoyance is poorly masked in my gritted response.

His eyes flare. "You crashed up your car. On the fucking highway in mid-pursuit. A highway full of other drivers. You disobeyed protocol and disappeared for twenty-four hours with Johnson, and there's yet to be a report on my desk—"

5

I nod to the file in my lap, eyebrows raised.

His face pinches. "You're leaving me no choice."

This gains my full attention. "No choice for what?"

Rubbing the back of his neck, he moves behind his desk and opens the top drawer. "Badge and gun." He thrusts his hand out. "I'm sorry, Quinn. But you're suspended from active duty until further notice."

I'm out of the chair and bracing my palms on the edge of his desk, giving myself an anchor to prevent me from doing something stupid. Like throwing the chair through the glass. "Don't do this. You know we don't have time for politics. Sir," I amend. "Avery's not out of danger yet, and there's a killer out there—"

Wexler sighs audibly. "Apparently, with my department, there's always someone in danger and always a perp out there killing." For a second, his features fall with despair, but he quickly pulls his hard captain persona back into place. "I have bosses, too, detective. And I'm taking it up the ass for the shit you pulled, so I need you out of here until it blows over. I promise, Avery will have the best detail on her at all times."

More than anything, Avery's safety is most important. I believe Wexler and the department have every intention of seeing to her safety, but I can't step aside on this.

Resigned, I suck in a breath and pull out my leather holder and lay my shield on his desk next to the report on Avery's abduction. Then I unclip my GLOCK from my shoulder harness and set it alongside them. A pressure hits my chest like a wrecking ball. I've never been thrown off a case before. Never been suspended. Over twenty years of duty with one of the cleanest records, and this is my reward.

One moment of panic where I feared losing the woman I care about—where for the first time, I let instinct override logic—has torn that all away.

I turn to make a dramatic exit. I don't regret a damn second that I put Avery first.

"Oh—and, Quinn?"

I pause with my hand latched to the door.

"Leave your notes on the case in your office. Good work on that. I'll get a team to take over."

My knuckles turn white as I grip the handle and crack the door open. "And Bonds?" I ask.

His groan clenches my teeth. "Send her in," he says. "She's next."

I close the door and turn toward the captain. "You can't take her off this case." I'm shocked the words have left my mouth. Just twenty-four hours ago, I was undecided on how involved I wanted Sadie, questioning whether or not I could ever trust my partner again.

There are many levels of trust, however. And right now, I trust that Sadie will do whatever it takes to protect Avery. What I don't trust is her method to see that through, and that's the struggle of this new murky-gray water I now find myself treading.

Wexler narrows his gaze. "She fired her weapon from

a moving vehicle on the highway." He says this like it's explanation enough. And really, the Ethan Quinn of just a month ago would've been the first to sign Sadie's dismissal papers for that action. But today, I'd give her that order all over again in a heartbeat to save Avery.

"Bonds was only following my directive," I say, lifting my chin. "I take full responsibility."

He shakes his head. "That's very admirable. But you know that's not how it works. Her weapon, her reprimand."

Remembering the last case and how well Bonds took *my* reprimand, I give Wexler a curt nod. Sadie will back off about as much as I will: not one bit. "Just know that Agent Bonds did what she had to in order to get Avery out of that van."

Eyebrows hiked, Wexler says, "This isn't personal, Quinn. *Doctor Johnson—*" he stresses, making me aware of my personal address of our department medical examiner "—is a part of our team. Everyone here is dedicated to protecting her and solving this case for her sake. You need to reevaluate your priorities. Gain some perspective."

With a deep inhale, nostrils flaring, I straighten my back. "No disrespect, captain. But when it comes to one of our own, it's very personal." I face the door and open it. "You know where I'll be when you need me."

Before I exit, he says, "I do need you on this as soon as possible. That's why I'm asking you to take some time to get your shit straight."

I close the door behind me before I make the mistake of

combating my superior. I've tarnished my reputation enough for one day. As I enter the bullpen, I can barely look Sadie in her jade green eyes. The betrayal she must have felt when I took her off the previous case resonates deeply.

"That bad?" she asks, tucking her hands into her back pockets.

I cross my arms, noting the empty feel of my missing gun. Sadie did her best to save my badge, but someone has to take the hit. It should be me. "I tried to take the brunt of it, but you're up now. Wexler wants to see you."

Worry creases the slim slope of her brow. I know her concern is not for herself, but there's no reason to tell her I'm off the case. She'll find out soon enough.

"I can handle it," she says, and I have no doubt she'll give Wexler her worst.

As she heads toward the captain, I face Avery and tick my chin in the direction of my office. I shut out the racket of the bullpen and lock the door, mentally cursing the glass walls that offer us no privacy. It's the first time since this morning that I've been alone with her, and I want nothing more than to touch her.

"What's happening, Quinn?" she asks. "I thought we had this worked out. Or, at least a starting point."

With my back to her, I pull the shades down, giving us the illusion of privacy, at least. "Politics," I answer as honestly as I can. When I turn toward her, the confused squint of her beautiful brown eyes pulls me to her side like a magnet.

9

Her scent of lavender invades my senses, searing my chest. I push out a long breath to clear my mind. "I've been suspended."

Avery shakes her head. "But they can't do that."

I release a clipped laugh. "Oh, they can and they have." I spear my fingers through my hair, annoyed with the fact that I can't just crush this woman to my chest. I've never felt this fucking vulnerable—and I hate the weak feeling arising from needing her this instant.

I back up a step and seek a breath not laced with her scent. "Suspended or not, off the case or not…it doesn't matter." I head around my desk and dig out my key ring to unlock the bottom drawer. "I'm not letting you out of my sight."

I gather copies of the documents I made and the flash drive with all my research. Wexler can have my files, but I'm taking the copies with me.

"I have to work, Quinn," Avery says, and I look up as she wraps her arms around herself. "I need to make sure the autopsy on the second victim is done right. Those men were testing that drug on those women." She absentmindedly touches her fingers to her mouth, her scar. "I have to find a connection to the drug and their deaths, and the second vic may have the evidence we need to make that connection."

I shut the drawer and slam my files on the desk. Anger seizes my thoughts before I have time to filter the words leaving my mouth. "Like fucking hell, you're working in this building. You've been abducted not once but *twice*, Avery. Right here, in the fucking ACPD building, with cops all around." I wave my hand for emphasis.

"Please don't patronize me." Her shoulders deflate, and a stab of guilt slices into my gut. "Are you suggesting someone here is working for the other side?"

I shake my head, exasperation creeping in. "Simon, your own lab tech, was…so yeah. I guess I am. I don't trust anyone here." I eye her closely. "Especially when it comes to your safety. You're not safe here, Avery."

Her eyes soften as her gaze flicks over my features. "You don't trust anyone. Not even Sadie?"

My mouth pops open, the words to counter that accusation right on the tip of my tongue, but I can't summon the conviction. "I trust Sadie to protect you."

Avery senses the ambiguity in that comment, but doesn't get to question me further. As if on cue, a rap sounds at my door. Sadie stands on the other side, her features creased in distress.

Shit.

"This isn't up for debate." I walk toward the door and unlock it. Avery's huff of frustration tenses my shoulders, and I'm not prepared for Sadie's blast as she powers past me.

Sadie takes a cross-armed stance in the middle of my office. "Were you planning to tell me you were off the case?"

Jesus. I'm surrounded by pissed off women. Where's Carson when I actually need him?

I close the door. "Nothing changes. We stick to the plan.

11

I'll be back on duty soon."

The plan was for Sadie and Carson to investigate Maddox and his law firm while Avery and I work the perps and evidence. That way, I could assure Avery's safety as we investigate her darknet connections. But since I'm no longer a welcome member of the team, or even a detective with a shield, that's out of the question.

I'll go fucking crazy worrying over Avery.

I face Sadie, firm in my decision. "Avery's going to take a leave of absence."

"No." Avery shakes her head, hands raised. "No, I'm not. I will not let those monsters get away with—"

"It's for the best," Sadie cuts in, and Avery's angry expression falls. Shock at the betrayal plainly displayed in the furrow of her brow. "You got away, Avery," Sadie continues. "But this isn't over. Not yet. You're being targeted."

For a brief second, Avery's features flash with alarm. She hides her panic quickly, rolling her shoulders back and lifting her head. "I'm not afraid of them."

Sadie's never been the most compassionate—hell, some days I wonder if she has a sympathetic bone in her body—but I'm onboard this time. Her bluntness is necessary to make Avery comprehend the level of danger she's in.

I address Sadie. "Are you still in?"

"I got saddled with backlogged parking tickets," she says. "So I'm not benched, if that's what you mean. I guess it could've been worse."

It could've been, but still, there's nothing pleasant about parking ticket duty. "We're still working the case." I glance between them. "I'm not officially, of course, but no one has any knowledge of your connections, Avery. That's an angle that's all ours, and we'll work it."

Sadie cranes an eyebrow. "Detective Quinn going outside the law?"

I lay a heavy glare on her. "Don't get so excited. I'm not going vigilante"—I narrow my gaze—"I'm just not above doing a little side sleuthing. I still want all updates on Maddox and that law firm. Anything you uncover at Lark and Gannet comes to me." I exhale heavily. "Keep me in the know until I'm back on the case."

Avery catches Sadie's notice, and some unsaid communication passes between them. "All right," Sadie says, shifting her stance. "Mission Black Hat Quinn in effect. I'll keep you posted." She heads out of my office, and I'm left with a strange wariness I can't place.

"Wondering how to begin again?"

I look at Avery, that heaviness on my chest damn near crushing me. "Yeah. Pretty much exactly."

She sidles up beside me and slips her hand into mine. I stare down as our fingers lace together. "Come on," she says, pulling me toward the door. "If we're going rogue, let's make it count."

CHAPTER 3

FRAYED

AVERY

*T*he *tap tap tap* of our footfalls echos like the secondhand of a clock ticking down. The rhythmic patter against the linoleum could lull me to sleep. I march down the white-walled corridor as if I've been zombiefied, a medical examiner's worst fear.

It's ironic, I guess. A hollowed out shell of a woman, a corpse in my own right, on my way to the morgue. If not for Quinn risking his career to save me, I'd most likely be on a slab in my own lab right now.

I don't know what would've happened if Quinn and Sadie hadn't been able to stop that van. But I know, eventually, those men would've killed me. It's not as if they were just going to let me walk away with their secrets.

Secrets.

They have one of mine, as well. And since I did escape, I wonder how long I have until Mr. A. K. Tie—the man who threatened me; the reason why I'll never forget the cold bite of steel inside me—makes my damning secret known.

But after the events of the past forty-eight hours, lethargy is my immediate enemy—the threat weighing me down with each exhausting step.

I could've put up more of a fight with Quinn, dug my heels in and refused to be removed from my lab, where I have control over the evidence as it's discovered. I could have—and I would've eventually worn him down, but the thought of resting was more tempting.

I want to laugh. Risk my life, my freedom, my reputation... for just one extra hour of sleep. But screw sleep. Sleep is my enemy, too.

Every second already lost will take hours to recover on this case.

I force my feet to keep moving forward, leading Quinn toward the crime lab. I'm hyperaware of him behind me, the press of his strong presence against my back. So when he grabs ahold of my wrist and pulls me into a nook along the hallway, I'm only slightly alarmed.

"What are you doing?" I look up into his face as he towers over me.

"We need to be on the same page." He's standing way too close, causing my heart to thump erratically in my chest.

I swallow hard. "We are, Quinn. I get it."

He trails his hand up my arm, grips my bicep, his worry evident in that one action. "Get your team on point, but don't give them any more information than needed."

My shoulders sag. I'm not sure what to respond to first. His obvious concern, or his domineering temperament. As my defenses surge, anger over my situation rising anew, I'm swayed toward defensive. "They're not idiots," I snap. "They have access to all the same evidence, and they need to know what to do with that evidence."

He releases a deep breath and removes his hand. "I meant about your circumstance. The only lead we have right now is your darknet connections. If someone in your lab gets wind of that…" He presses his lips together. "I don't want anything leaked to the press. I don't want these people you've been dealing with to get spooked and disappear."

"What makes you think it's my department leaking?"

His eyebrows hike toward his gray-streaked hairline. "There have now been two incidents within your department. Simon was a damn serial killer, and—"

"And those men who barged into my lab yesterday have nothing to do with my people." My jaw sets stubbornly. Although, there's nothing I can offer in way of Simon's excuse. I'm still not sure how Price Wells got to him; whether Simon was a part of Wells' plan from the beginning and then infiltrated my lab, or if Wells selected him after the fact.

Either way, it doesn't matter. Quinn's right. The crime lab is tainted. A monster like Wells took one look at my lab and found a weakness, an opening. How many others in here—in this building—are just as weak and waiting for a moment to snap.

I shake my head. "I'm sorry. You're right."

Quinn moves closer. His body heat charges the air, igniting a craving to be touched. "I don't want to be right," he says. "I just want to make sure no one else gets hurt."

The depth of his words buries me in yearning. And when he palms my cheek, the rough pads of his fingers tracing my face, I wish I could make that promise to him.

There's a gulf between us, dividing us further apart with every passing second. When he finally knows the truth of me, what I'm capable of and what I've done...it won't be my pain that I wish I could vanquish.

Before I'm able to entertain the thought of pressing my lips to his, he pulls away. "Let's get the facts we need, then put this sting together."

I nod, run my hands over my shirt and pull the hem straight. Soon, I won't be able to protect Quinn from my secrets. Those secrets will rip through our tentative feelings for each other with a fury, decimating not only us, but whatever faith he has left in the law.

That kills me.

I don't want to be the one to tear his conviction away.

As we move through the hallway, the fluorescent lights above wash the world in bleached out colors, as if I'm trapped in some realm between sleep and wakefulness. The fatigue becomes all-consuming. My head is thick with a dense cotton feel, like I'm teetering on the verge of sickness.

It's futile to fight against the impending illness, though. The sickness has already invaded me. The day I agreed to help dispose of Price Wells, my abductor, was the day I welcomed it in with open arms.

Simon's not the only one who taints this place.

As I push the swing doors open, heads turn my way, eyes wide and staring openly. My lab techs freeze in place. I can see it in their shocked expressions: the questions. *Why am I here? How badly was I damaged this time?* And the one pressing fear none of them will voice but screams from their eyes: *are they next?*

"Do you want me to—?" Quinn begins.

"No." I stop him short. "I can handle this." Returning the first time was damn impossible. This time, however, is not like starting over. Not like finding my rhythm again and trying to put the past behind me.

There's an unnerving thread of panic tightening around me and flowing like a current through this room, warning me that this is only the start.

"Natalie." I approach my intern, and she's quick to try to make me feel at ease before I can get my instructions out.

"Doctor Johnson. Oh, my God, we were so worried about you. Are you all right?" Her large dark eyes beg to hear a lie— any lie. One that will alleviate her worries.

My lips turn up in a tight smile. "I'm fine. Thank you. I'm

not at liberty to discuss the details…" I glance at Quinn, and he nods assuredly. "But it's important that we go over a few things. The autopsy reports need to be corrected, and I need you to report all evidence and findings to me."

While I instruct the lab on the two victims and correct the COD reports, Quinn takes a call from Sadie. I can barely focus as I try to eavesdrop. This second, Sadie is in the very place where my abductor used to work. Did Wells sit at a desk and plot his scenes? Choose his methods and dream about them while talking to his clients? How can Sadie even step foot in that law firm?

My hand spasms over the keyboard and I flex my fingers.

"Doctor Johnson?"

I shake out my hand. "Lauren Carter," I say, directing Natalie's attention to the COD report. "Was brought in yesterday, but still needs to be properly identified. I want a full autopsy and toxicology. I want the reports done thoroughly, but delivered to me as soon as possible."

Quinn moves off to the side of the lab, talking in a heated, lowered tone. I latch on to his voice, allowing it to anchor me in the present. It keeps me from fixating on what occurred in the spot I'm now standing.

I can still feel the cold steel of the gun. My legs tremble as I force the crude memory from my mind and instead focus on the screen.

"I'm glad you're taking some time off," Natalie says.

I almost laugh. As if I didn't just return from time off.

Maybe Quinn's right—maybe moving my department to another floor, closer to the ACPD, isn't such a bad idea.

"My leave won't be long," I assure her. "Please, just keep me updated on everything in the meantime."

The door to my office is unlocked, and a sinking feeling pulls at my stomach as I enter. Things are just as I left them yesterday, only it somehow feels different. Off. Like this isn't my office at all.

"Do you need help?" Quinn stands at the doorway.

I push my hair back from my face and turn toward my desk. "Just need my laptop and a few files. I have mostly everything we need on my computer at home."

"We'll grab that, too. Along with whatever else you'll need."

Confusion pushes my brows together as I face him. "Grab my stuff...to go where?"

Abashed doesn't suit Quinn. The way he shifts his stance, shoves his hands into the pockets of his slacks. His gaze, though—that is steady on me as his lips thin into a determined line. "You're staying with me."

My mouth parts, disbelief shocking me silent.

"It's not safe at your house," he continues, pulling his hands from his pockets and lacing his arms over his broad chest, effectively setting his body language in a deflective, no argument stance.

I take my own defensive measures, propping my fists on my hips. "Now you're crossing a line, Quinn. I'm sorry, but I won't be made to feel so...helpless. My home is the one place where—" I break off, searching for the right words. "It's *my* place. It's the only place I have left that this darkness can't touch me."

His whole body tenses, his nostrils flare. And in the second his tough persona slips, I glimpse the crack in his armor that conveys pain.

Shit. I might as well have slapped him. My mouth flies open to correct myself—to let him know that I didn't mean… Hell, I don't know what I meant. Yes, I feel safe with Quinn. But I don't want to feel dependent on that. On him.

The nights he spent holding my hand while I slept, fitfully, in that hospital bed come rushing back, and I'm suddenly mortified. No matter where I am, he's my haven.

And he wants me.

"I have to have something of my own," I try, sensing my backpedaling making it worse. God, what's wrong with me? "You understand that, right?"

He steps forward, closing the door behind him with a loud *click*. "You understand that the people who took you yesterday know who you are. As much as this pains me to say, you have to hear it, Avery. They had no intention of releasing you. You know too much, and they're not just going to let you—"

"Live?"

A heavy breath expels. "Exactly. But I promise. We'll figure this out and end it so you can put it behind you."

I want to scream. Maybe even cry. Yet another thing to put behind me. When does it end? What if I'd just refused to

21

correct the drug. Trifecta—that's what the man in the mask called it. Had I'd just stood my ground and denied them that, then they would've killed me, and this would already be over. No more running. No more fear.

No more secrets and no more lies.

The truth hovers on my tongue, a breath away from confessing my sins. Quinn needs to know—I have to tell him everything in the hope that he can glean even one clue to stop this madness.

Yet, in life's never-ceasing moments of irony, my phone rings, dragging me from the depths of panic. I gulp down a breath to expand my burning lungs and glance at my phone. Detective Carson's name flashes on the screen. "Johnson," I answer, raising my gaze to Quinn.

"I heard you were taking a leave of absence," Carson says. "Is that true?"

I rub my forehead, my thoughts muddled. "Uh, yes. I am. Why?"

A brief few seconds of silence, then: "Shit. I need to know who to contact, then," Carson says. "Another body has been reported. A victim that needs processing—"

"I'm on my way." I still have the phone to my ear as I head toward my locker.

"But I thought you were off? Avery, you can hand this over—"

"Carson," I snap, then squeeze my eyes closed briefly and curb the irritation in my voice. "I said I'm going. Is there a mark? On the vic's thigh?"

As Carson goes on about just being called away from the law firm, Quinn steps into my line of sight. "Give me the phone."

I hesitate. "Why?"

"So I can tell Carson you're *not* going."

I hold Quinn's unwavering stare. "Carson, please pick me up a coffee and I'll meet you there in five." I end the call and turn to my locker, yanking out a jacket and pair of pants. "I don't want to hear it, Quinn. This is bigger than me and you, and I need to go."

He flattens his palm against the wooden door, caging me in. "I know." I pivot enough to meet his gaze. "I know what that demanding pull feels like. I just… Fuck."

His hand slams against the door, and I flinch. This isn't only about his desire to protect me; he *needs* to be there, to do his job, and he can't. I rest my hand on his strong forearm. "You didn't get the update."

He glances down at the silent phone clipped to his belt. "Removed from the case, remember?" A dejected, tight smile fights free. "So another vic turned up. Another woman, possibly another pro." Quinn lowers his hand, slipping away from my touch, and I resume sliding on my medical examiner jacket. "I guess it would be futile to point out this might be an effort to lure you out."

Actually, I hadn't thought about that at all. "I'll be safe." I yank my skirt down to change into the pants. Quinn averts his gaze, always the gentlemen.

"Nothing you haven't seen before. Recently, in fact." This forces his eyes on me, and I wink.

"There's a time and place, and this isn't it." He moves closer as I pull my pants over my hips. "But that doesn't mean I haven't thought about you constantly since this morning." He snags the drawstrings of my pants and tugs me forward, his mouth hovering near mine, too close, as he loops the strings together and cinches the waist tight.

My breath catches, my whole body alert, as I await the press of his lips.

He rests his hands on my hips and lowers his mouth to my ear. "I want an update every hour, and your detail goes everywhere you go. This isn't up for debate."

I blink. My breathing struggles to regulate and sync with my rapid heartbeats. "I can live with that."

He inclines his head to the side, his gaze roams my face. "Good." Then his hand slides into my hair as he presses a tender kiss to my forehead. He backs away, leaving me chasing the fire in my belly. "I'll be there in a second if you need me."

A small smile stretches my lips. "I know. Thank you."

Quinn may have difficulty expressing himself when it comes to matters of the heart…which I can't fault him. We're both clumsily maneuvering this thing between us. But when it comes to his job, he *is* the job.

"Oh, here," I say, heading toward my desk. I tweak a sheet of paper from a notepad and jot down my ID and passwords.

"This will give you access to the darknet under my account." I hand him the paper. "While I'm identifying the newest victim, maybe you can figure out how those bastards found me."

He accepts my keys as I place them in his hand. A crease burrows between his brows. "Just like that. You're giving me access."

I shrug. "I trust you."

Our eyes stay locked as the weight of that statement presses upon the span of air between us. "And I trust that you know how to operate the interface," I add, turning to grab my bag. "You said that you once worked a case where you had to learn more than the basics, so I don't think you'll mess anything up. Too much."

His chuckle is light, and in stark contrast to our current situation. A testament to how much we've already endured. "You were listening."

"Had to do something to keep myself from tearing your clothes off and jumping your bones." I cock my head and grin, loving how this tough man, who has faced down numerous bad guys, flushes at my words.

"All right," I say, anchoring the strap over my shoulder. "Here we go."

"Wait."

That's the only warning I'm given before Quinn grasps my waist and hauls me against the wall. He presses me into the corner, his mouth finding mine in the same beat that I gasp. His lips are hard and demanding, his tongue delves deep to taste me as his hands roam beneath my shirt to steal a rough caress of my flesh.

I can't help it; I moan into the kiss, unable to control the longing. I'm terrified—terrified of leaving this office and confronting fears that threaten me with all my suffering. I cling to his strong shoulders, losing myself in a moment of weakness.

When he breaks away, his labored breaths coming as fast as my own, he whispers, "I should come with you."

As much as I want that very thing…again, I can't allow myself to become dependent on Quinn's protection. "Wexler would have a shit-fit if you showed up at the crime scene."

His expression contorts. "Right."

I wish I knew how to make this better for him. For Quinn, being suspended must feel close to death. I run my hand up the back of his neck, kissing him slowly before saying, "I'll call every hour. We will figure this out."

He licks his lips as he pulls back and holds up my keys. "You'll know where I'll be. Come on. I'll follow you there first."

I watch him leave my office, taking a moment to collect myself before I'm able to face my lab. There's another body, another dead girl. And this time, I know she didn't die in pursuit of the Trifecta serum.

If the Alpha Killer is trying to send a message, it's been received.

CHAPTER 4

CROSSHAIR

QUINN

very's scent lingers in the air of her bedroom; the fragrance of lavender and vanilla mingles with a faint antiseptic trace of the crime lab. It tightens my chest, knowing she's too far away. Tucking my unease down deep, I make quick work of locating her suitcase and packing essential items.

I have half the department keeping an eye on her at the crime scene, but that does little to ease my nerves. If she wants to go off alone, she'll find a way. I shove a toiletry bag with her toothbrush and other necessities into the case, forcing myself to stay calm. The less she has to worry over, the easier it will be for her to accept. She has to be with someone at all times until this is over.

And putting her up at my place will ensure no one will get to her. What I can't control is her own damn lab. For that, I'll have to trust Sadie. As uneasy as it makes me, I know she's the only one who I can count on to keep Avery covered.

Once I've made a thorough mess, having lost my patience and strewn clothes around the room, I huff a defeated breath and place her suitcase next to the door. I'll clean up later. But first, I need to find her laptop.

The interface is easy enough to navigate. I click my way through logging in and locating her contacts. I do a quick search for any screen names or pseudonyms that might be associated with Maddox. It's a slim chance, I know, but I've still got it bad for that lawyer. I'm not sure how dirty he is—whether or not his services to his clients extend to acquiring rare drug ingredients such as ambergris—but I know he isn't squeaky clean.

Proving it will be the difficult part. With a firm like Lark and Gannet backing him, and his campaign running for the Commonwealth, Maddox has built a solid wall around himself.

If I discover he had even the slightest role in Avery's abduction, he'll need a hell of a lot more than that to protect him. Finding no red flags around Maddox, I end the search and pull up her last correspondence. It's basic. A simple order and scheduled drop, where Avery would pick up the ambergris.

I push back in the chair, my gaze glossing over the details. I should be at the crime scene with Avery and my team. Every second and every bit of evidence is sensitive, and needs to be analyzed on site. I look at my phone and open the last received message.

Avery: *Just meeting up with Carson now. Nothing to report yet—I'll keep you posted.*

Dragging my hands down my face, I stare at the laptop screen. Fuck it. I'm not on duty. I have no one to answer to. I type out a message to FalconStar10, Avery's ambergris hookup, and hit Send. Then I take the laptop with me as I head to the door.

Before I leave, I grab the one picture frame on the mantel. It's been turned facedown. I noticed it the first night I was here, when I was searching for any trace of Avery's family, people she could turn to. I open the back of the frame and take out the picture of Avery.

Her brown eyes stare at me, her lips creased in an easy smile. It must've been taken when she first moved here; her first day as the new lead medical examiner. I pocket the picture in my jacket inseam and head out.

The drop is a small coffee shop on the corner of Wilson and Barton. It's an intimate setting, unlike the big coffee franchises, and the perfect place to organize a meet. Avery did good. She's smart, picking a public place, but not too busy where a person might overlook a meet gone bad.

I've been parked in front of Bean Friends for ten minutes, waiting for Mister Falconstar. Since Avery already knows what he looks like, I couldn't ask that he sport a red baseball cap. I have to go on instincts.

I recline back in the driver-seat, prop my hands on the steering wheel. I had just enough time to drop Avery's stuff at my apartment and grab a shower and change clothes before making the meet.

With a huff, I reach down and unclip my phone. I read over Avery's last update, again trying to decipher her state of mind, and anything that could clue me in on what's happening.

Avery: *All evidence points to the same offender. No ID on the vic yet. I'll have more once the vic is taken to the lab and processed.*

My detective Spidey senses are tingling. The vagueness of her report has me damn near forgetting this whole meet and heading straight to Wexler and demanding to be put back on the case. Especially since the two perps we arrested yesterday have their bond hearing in a couple of hours. If Maddox gets his clients out on bond and they walk for now...

Anger spikes my blood at the thought. That won't happen. Captain won't let that happen. But I should be the one to take the first crack at questioning those fuckers.

The past two days feel like an eternity; no down time to think. And now, as I sit in the silence of my car, my brain won't stop thinking—thinking about what those fucks had planned for Avery after injecting her with the drug.

I grip the wheel hard, my knuckles breaking the newly healed skin.

Avery was out of her mind with lust. Suffering, in agony,

the only way to relieve her torment was to achieve sexual release. If a synthetic drug like that hits the streets, if that's what the intent is behind all this, the world will become a rapist's playground.

My stomach roils with my mounting fury, and I know that no matter what, we have to stop that from happening.

Before my thoughts can swallow me, plunging me to the pit of my own plagued mind, I spot a guy with a dark backpack making his way toward the coffee shop. He doesn't go in. He looks around a few times before settling at one of the outside tables.

That's my guy.

I leisurely get out of my car and cross the street, keeping him in my peripheral as I head toward the front doors. I'm not even a foot away when the guy makes me. He bounds out of the chair and he's off.

Dammit. I really didn't feel like chasing him down. I pick up my pace and then break into a run once I round the corner of the building. He just reaches the middle of the alley when I catch up to him.

"Stop! Police!" I go to reach for my badge and curse as I feel inside my empty pocket. No gun, either. Why the fuck did I even strap on my holster? With a growl, I push forward, legs pumping, and snatch the collar of his shirt, taking him down to the pavement.

"I said police, dipshit." My breath is ragged as I pull his arms behind his back and secure a pair of cuffs to his wrists.

At least I have those.

"Where's your badge?" he fires back.

Looks like he's no first-time offender; he knows the deal. I roll him over and stare down. "It's in my other pants."

"Fuck," he hisses. "You a nark?"

Catching my breath, I rest my hands on my thighs. My age is showing. Hell. "Why the fuck would a nark try to make a collar?" He obviously isn't that smart. "What's in the bag?"

He clams up, refusing to answer any questions.

All right. I yank his pack to the side of his shoulder and unzip the top. I pull out a baggie of pot and shake it in front of his face. "What's this?" Then I tug out a large foil-wrapped rock. I assume that's Avery's package. "And looks like you got a rock here, too."

"Hey, man. That's not the kind of rock you're thinking."

I peel back a section of the foil and give it a whiff. "Actually, it's exactly what I think. Ambergris."

He squints at me, a deep furrow between his dark brows. "You FDA?"

"I'm your worst fucking nightmare if you don't tell me everything." I yank him up by his shirt into a sitting position. "Talk."

Shit-for-brains can't possibly be in collusion with Maddox and the masked men who took Avery. Those men are career criminals, and this guy looks like he'd piss himself if they so much as whistled his way for a dime bag. "This the biggest score you got?" I ask.

His embarrassment is evident on his youthful face. "Yeah, man. The dope's mine. Personal use. I got a prescription for my migraines."

"Sure. All right. I'll let you off the hook with that." I kneel down and push the ambergris in his face and tug out the photo of Avery. "Now tell me everything about this shit here and this woman."

"I just got the hookup for that chick, is all. My cousin's in the Navy." He shrugs, wincing at the movement. "He sends me the rocks, and I get them to her. I saw her posting on a forum trying to score some. And I actually knew what she was looking for." He grins wide. "I remembered my cousin talking about how that shit could go for a lot to the right person." He shrugs again. "It was fate."

I let him talk. Most people will tell you what you want to know without even asking if you let them talk long enough. And he's a talker.

"Anyone else on that forum trying to locate it?" I ask.

"Naw, man. Just the hot chick." His smile stretches, revealing gold dental plates. "I was actually going to try to hook up with her today. Bitch has a fine fucking ass."

My jaw sets. I thump the back of his head. "Focus, shithead. Anyone else ever approach you, inquiring about ambergris or this woman?"

"Damn, man. That's police brutality." He shakes his head. "I said no. Just her."

I mutter a curse and move behind him to unlock the cuffs.

If I was on duty, I'd bring him in, put him in the hotbox for proper questioning. Sweat all the details out. But I have a feeling he'd only waste time and resources. Time and resources we don't have.

The kind of scores he gets through his cousin doesn't seem big enough to tempt the real players in this game. According to Avery, the men who took her had a whole lab set up—with enough illegal pure drugs to dope the entire city.

They have their own connections—but they still needed a talented scientist.

"Oh, wait though," he says, rubbing his wrist. "There was this one dude, kind of sketchy. He asked her a question on the forum. Something about the compounds and aphrodisiacs. It got all technical between them."

I toss his backpack to him once I'm done searching it. "You're just now remembering this?" He scratches at his head, shrugs. "And what stood out about that to you?"

"I don't know. I guess because it was a drug forum. People looking to get innovative ways to get high. You know, for SWIM." He nods a couple of times, looking proud of himself for using the right slang. This twerp doesn't have a clue what he's fucking around with.

"What – your mommy bought you the darknet for Christmas?" I wave him on, impatient. "And?"

"And it just didn't fit. I mean, the girl sure. I could tell she was legit and just looking for some hard-to-get shit. But him? It was like he was looking for *her*. You know what I'm saying?"

I do. Even a moron like this kid can read between the lines.

"You don't start a convo with a chick about aphrodisiacs without having an ulterior motive," he finishes with a shit-eating grin.

I'm impressed he strung that sentence together.

And Avery, even the brainy scientist she is, didn't pick up on that. She doesn't think like a criminal. Or hell, like a man.

"What's this guy's screen name?"

He stands and dusts off his backside. "I get a reward for this or some shit?"

I step up to him and glare down, letting our sizable difference speak for itself.

"Fuck," he mutters. "All right, just don't give my name over to any of your nark buddies or cops, and I'll tell you. It was King."

I raise my eyebrows. "King?"

"Yeah, I'm trying to think. It was A. King or something." He holds up his hands. "But I can get it for you for sure when I get back to my house."

"I know you will, Laurence," I say, handing him the driver's license I snaked from his pack. "You'll send it to this number here"—I give him my card—"or else I'll bring my cop buddies to your house and have us a fun search party."

"Man." He shakes his head, exasperated. "I'll send it, yo."

"Send it within the hour."

When I'm back at my car, I text Avery, inquiring about this King contact she might recall. I wait a few minutes, my restlessness mounting when she doesn't respond. Frustration laces my nerves tight as I crank the engine and head toward my apartment. That just happens to be near the crime scene.

CHAPTER 5

AFFLICTION

AVERY

'Ve lost it. My ability to cope, to reason, to breathe. Bile coats my throat, my stomach roils with a sick tumble, and pain lances my chest. The bright day burns through my eyelids, too bright, too vivid. White circles flicker at the edges of my vision as I squeeze my eyes closed.

"Avery?"

I bend at the waist, gasp for air, dragging searing breaths into my constricted lungs. "I'm fine. Just give me a minute," I tell Carson.

"Quinn's going to have my ass if I don't report this…"

I hold up a hand. "Not yet." I manage to right myself and clear my thoughts of the victim. She's behind me now, being photographed. Becoming a grotesque work of crime scene art.

"I'm processing this victim," I say, overly determined, as if giving myself a pep talk. "It's just exhaustion catching up.

I'll get a second wind soon. Quinn doesn't need to know." I find Carson's gaze, and he nods reluctantly. Quinn will do something completely caveman—like storm the scene and throw me over his shoulder. Hell, he's done it before.

Carson offers me my coffee, but I shake my head. "I think the caffeine had an adverse effect." Thankfully, he accepts the lame attempt to excuse my sudden attack.

We both know the truth. The sight and *smell* of the vic hit too hard. Not right at first; shock might've staved it off. But once I was there beside her, visualizing and feeling her last moments…the panic took hold. Gripping me like death grips her now.

"I could call Bonds over here," Carson says, worry creasing his eyes. "She could give us some insight into the offender, maybe, and—" *And hold my hand*, I surmise for him.

As if everyone here isn't already thinking about how damaged I am and questioning whether I can do this. Whether I *should* do this. I don't need a profiler here to add weight to their concerns.

I'm my own boss, and I'm a responsible one. I did get clearance from my department psychologist on the way here. She wanted me to come in, but after I explained the importance of this case, she reluctantly cleared me. This case is my priority.

"No. It's fine." I roll my shoulders back and flick my bangs out of my eyes. Suck down another crisp, fall-laced breath that doesn't reek of the vic.

Though having Sadie here would benefit the case—there

are areas where she excels beyond Carson, and even Quinn—it's better if she's not. I've become too dependent even on Sadie. Besides, her being at Lark and Gannet, asking the tough questions, means no one else has to.

I have to push through. If I give in now, if I let fear drive me, then I'm doing exactly what those bastards want.

That was their intent when they dressed the vic in *my* lab coat.

"Instruct the unis away from the vic," I tell Carson, grateful he's the on-scene detective in Quinn's absence. He listens well without questioning or reading too much into my every statement.

As he clears CSU and the uniforms away from the scene, I bring out my recorder and steady my voice as I recite the date and time. "Victim is a Caucasian female between the age of twenty and twenty-five." I pause the device and scrutinize her hips to be more certain. They're narrow and from what I can see, hold no definitive proof to whether she's given birth in her lifetime.

The age is an educated guess based on that fact, but with what I have to work with…it's the best I can do until I can examine her further.

"Cause of death appears to be—" Torture. Extreme, sadistic torture. "Maltreatment. Varying depths of lacerations to the outer longitudinal layer indicate the offender used a blade, possibly four-to-six inches, to remove the dermis from the victim's body. Significant perimortem blood loss suggests the victim was still alive during the removal of her skin."

I hit Pause and wipe my forehead with the sleeve of my jacket. Carson sends me a concerned glance, then adjusts his coat, flipping the collar up against the wind.

I clear my throat and kneel next to the victim. This is about how close I got before the attack took my breath. I haven't needed camphor ointment since I was in training, and I feel pathetic as I dig through my kit to find an old tub of Vics VapoRub that I keep around for the interns. I remove a glove and dab a bit of the cool, minty salve beneath my nose.

With my gloved hand, I peel back the white lab coat—the coat I was wearing yesterday when I was taken from my lab. I know it's mine before I even check the inseam, because there's a chocolate stain on the pocket from where I brushed my hand.

"I don't want to freak you out," Carson says, pulling my attention away from the vic. "But she kind of looks like you, Avery. I mean, in general. Blond hair. Close to your height and similar in build. And she's wearing the same kind of coat you do. Did she work in the crime lab…or do you think it could be a message?"

This is not a message. It's a threat.

The sight beneath the coat makes Carson curse, and I can only stare. Unsure of what I'm feeling. Numb, edgy, nauseated. Definitely nauseated. I've examined countless bodies, some in worse states than this. But not many. As a doctor, I have little sympathy; only aware I need to find the evidence to uncover her death. As a human being—the part of me I lock away so it's not touched by this kind of horror—is absolutely horrified.

"I'm not sure yet," I answer. "I don't think she was employed in the lab or the building. But I can't say that positively. Only that I've never laid eyes on her before."

And I have tried to place her. I remember that woman being hauled into the dank, greenly fluorescent-lit room by the masked man with a gun. Her knotted dark hair and sullen eyes. Her tearstained makeup smeared across her face. Was this victim—this woman—in the next room? Was she one of the women being doped and experimented on? Now that the masked man—if he was in fact the *boss*—has the perfected drug, did he do away with his test subjects since he no longer needs them?

My stomach bottoms out. I thought I was being brave when I tried to save that woman from being injected. When I took her place and was injected with the serum, instead. I didn't think; I reacted. And it never occurred to me that by correcting the drug, I was issuing a death sentence to others...

"Avery." Carson's concerned voice breaks through my flaring panic, and I shake myself out of my morbid thoughts.

I press Record. "The victim's breasts were excoriated from her body, probably with the same bladed instrument used to flay the dermis. The jagged, grooved pattern carved into the muscle and nicks to the breastbone indicate the offender applied a saw-like motion to amputate the breasts from the torso." I squeeze the device, aware of the trembling in my hand. "Other contusions mar the victim's face, but the face was left otherwise in tact, unscathed. Below the naval, patches of skin and muscle were abraded from the bones. Mutilated genitalia and other injuries inflicted upon the pubic region could indicate sexual trauma. Need further analysis to confirm."

"Time of death?" Carson prompts.

"Oh—" I restart the recorder. "Core body temperature was ninety-two point eight degrees upon initial examination. Estimated time of death is determined to be between three to five hours prior." I glance at my phone. "Between six and nine a.m. Approximately," I amend.

Subconsciously, I may have avoided calculating the time of death formula. The vic died not long ago…and her beastly, extensive injuries took hours to achieve. She suffered. She suffered excruciating torture like no human ever should.

I begin collecting samples, bagging any noticeable trace, as Carson crouches near. "So the lab coat. And the skin flaying. None of this really matches the previous vics. Could be to hide the fact they wanted to remove the mark or brand on the thigh; make this look like a different perp." He gestures toward the vic's leg, his features strained at the gruesome sight. "Any way to determine if she did in fact have a brand?"

"There may be," I say, but I don't need to examine the surrounding muscle tissue for evidence of a brand. The evidence that this was done by the same suspect who killed the first two vics…and who hurt me…doesn't need to be found within the victim.

She's wrapped in it.

I want Quinn's input on that, however, before I confirm with anyone else on the team.

"You have any insight into what the perp was thinking when they did this?"

I blow out a long breath. "I'm not a behaviorist, Carson. Sorry. I can only give you the facts as to her death, and the likeliness of the murder weapon."

"Right. I know that." He glances around, as if looking for something, or someone.

I realize then that he's pretty much on his own, and a swell of shame slams into me. I'm used to working by myself. I prefer it that way, actually. Carson, on the other hand, has probably never had to head up a crime scene on his own. And with Quinn out for blood, having been not-so-gently removed from the case, Carson most likely feels a lot of pressure not to fuck this up.

"Hey." When he turns my way, I lighten my tone. "I do think the chances of this being the same suspect, or *suspects*, is good. Better than good." I eye my coat. "Though I can't say this with any degree of certainty…with this level of overkill, the perp is likely a sadist. Possibly even of the psychopathic variety."

Maybe Sadie should be called in. As a high-functioning sociopath herself, Sadie would have perfect insight into this assailant's profile. A twinge of guilt nudges my conscience. The traits that help her identify psychopaths are also the attributes that helped her eradicate my abductor.

Carson watches me closely, and I add, "The offender either caught the vic by surprise, a blitz attack, or she was drugged. Possibly a combination of both. She has no defensive wounds." I glance down, sickened. "But then again, I may find some deep tissue bruising once I examine her."

"Noted," he says, literally noting my inferior guesswork down in his black notepad.

"This may be part of the scheme, throwing us off their scent, but the handiwork looks like one of a sexual sadist. Or at least, that's what he wants us to think. And if I had to make an educated guess as to the reasoning behind the brutal torture compared to the first two vics... More than the fact that he or they did enjoy their work, I'd wager the second part was misdirection."

His eyebrows draw together over his youthful features. "Misdirection? From what?"

I press my lips together, considering the real threat. While my colleagues are busy trying to protect me, no one is focusing on what's being hidden. "If we're chasing a killer, we're chasing ghosts." At his confused expression, I say, "We need to be chasing the living. The women that are still alive."

Understanding dawns, and he nods his head slowly. "This is the part I'm purposely being kept in the dark about."

A stab of shame pierces my chest. I don't know how much to reveal, how much to involve Carson, now that Quinn is no longer leading the case. "I'm sure you'll be brought up to speed soon," I say, trying and failing to encourage him.

"It's all right." He stands, brushing his hands down his slacks. "I made my bed. Guess I'll have to lie in it until I can prove myself."

Confusion forces me to my feet, questions as heavy as lead on the tip of my tongue. Before I'm able to voice them, Carson's attention is pulled toward another detective storming the scene.

"Phillips, where have you been? What do you got?" Carson fires off as the detective approaches.

The detective is momentarily distracted by the sight of the body. His dark features contort. "Jesus," he says.

I pack away the samples and my kit; I've done all I can here. I try not to think about the transport van that will soon be arriving. Just get back to the lab and focus on work.

"The FBI have been called in," Phillips announces, triggering both Carson and me to swap glances.

"Yeah, that was expected," Carson says, recovering quickly.

We knew Sadie would be reaching out to Special Agent Rollins. But really, this is a rather rapid response—considering it was only a fishing expedition on her part. The Alpha Omega crime ring is believed to be an urban legend within the criminal justice departments. I assumed Agent Rollins would blow off her inquiry.

"Expected? The FBI taking over was expected?" Phillips glares at Carson. "And were the two other bodies expected, too?"

A cold sensation prickles my skin, encasing me in sick dread.

Carson is already calling in to the precinct. "Captain—" He's cut off, and all I can do is hold my breath, awaiting to hear my fears confirmed.

The other women.

Detective Phillips sidles up beside me, his tall and stocky presence a shield against the biting wind.

"Who was called in?" I ask him. Sadie's call to Special Agent Rollins couldn't have done all this. Not when I heard it was Special Agent Proctor leading the charge on the last case.

His sigh is heavy. "Organized Crime Division." His dark eyebrows hike. "How's that for fucked irony? Pardon my French, but the other reports didn't even make it to us. The damn FBI intercepted them first. Big Brother politics." He shakes his head.

I turn toward him, while still trying to hear pieces of Carson's conversation. "What report was intercepted?"

He leans in, lowers his voice. "This wasn't the main attraction." He nods toward the victim. "The captain put us on this scene while the FBI took over the others. Probably to keep any link among them out of the press."

A sinking feeling burrows beneath my feet, like crashing waves dragging me into sand. And when Carson mutters into his phone and ends the call, I know before he even finds my eyes.

"It's official," Carson says. "The case has just been upgraded to a serial killer hunt. Sorry, Avery. Looks like we're chasing those ghosts."

CHAPTER 6

WHORE

ALPHA

My mother was a whore.

I remember the stench of filthy sex in our little rank, dirty apartment. It permeated the air, mingled with the sour stink of curdled milk left out on the counter and the moldy scent of old carpet and rain-ruined wallpaper.

I recall the groaning sounds coming from behind her bedroom door. Trying to silence the infuriating cries by cranking the volume of my cartoons on the small, static-lined TV. The muffled sobs when one of her johns got too violent.

Some sounds can't be drowned out.

Or forgotten.

It's the glare on the television that brings this memory racing back. There was always an annoying glare from the sun-bleached windows that never had any shutters. The first thing I did when I got my own place was put up blinds.

"Shut the fucking curtains."

Donavan does as instructed, and my hand relaxes on the remote as the widescreen display becomes crisp and vibrant in the dimmed room. I inhale a deep breath, taking in the fresh scent of leather and oleander. A combination that reminds me nothing of my mother's home.

As I knew they would, the press have sunk their greedy teeth into the serial killer epidemic. The media's appetite is insatiable, easily fed. The craze inflamed. Give them the bait, and they gnaw at the hook until their gums bleed.

The FBI have arrived. Not that they needed to make a special trip. They have a convenient office just outside of Arlington, the proverbial heart of the state. The press reporting the FBI's interception of the Alpha Killer case that, just today, was upgraded to serial killer status, means my pretties have been discovered.

I did so try to display my girls in a true sadistic art form.

And oh, how I enjoy watching them all scramble. Fumbling with their little clues.

The coppery tang of blood still lingers on my hands. When you spill so much, it's impossible to wash it all away.

I dig the tip of my finger into the pint of chocolate ice-cream, pop my finger into my mouth. Savor the metallic aftertaste of a job well done. Though I do take pride in my work, that's all it is: a job. There's little pleasure to be found in the demoralization of an empire.

A whimper steals my solitude, and I set the pint down and mute the TV.

I saved one of my treasures for the party. I have to have something to show for my hard work. She enters now, escorted roughly by her arms, Donavan and Micah directing her to kneel before me.

She's not the prize that I ultimately, intimately wanted, but... How did Dr. Lecter phrase it? *All good things to those who wait.*

Such irony, really. To quote a fictitious serial killer amid the current circumstances. Rather fitting, in a sort of cheap way. There is always humor to be found, though. Even in the blackest of souls.

And I am patient. My lovely medical examiner will make the perfect reward.

The lithe creature before me shies away as I reach for her. I latch on to her jaw and jerk her face forward. "If you struggle"—I tilt her quivering chin up—"I'll make this far more entertaining than it has to be."

Ready with the syringe, Donovan moves closer. I accept the serum with one hand as I hold the whore with the other. Her shaky whimpers slither over my skin as she extends a trembling arm outward.

"Good girl." I release her face only to grip her wrist and inject the needle deep into her forearm.

She bites back a scream. More from the shock than the pain. I imagine how the burn courses her blood, heating her from the inside out, as I push the plunger down.

She's glassy-eyed in a matter of seconds, barely able to put up a fight if she so desired. Which now, as she rolls her head, body becoming languid, demonstrates her desires have become anything I wish.

That's the beauty of it.

To all our desires, we are slaves. One must only know how to conquer these desires in order to fully possess another.

I rarely quote one of the greats if I can't do them justice— but what the hell? A little butchering never hurt anyone. That is, unless you're literal in your butchering.

"Those who restrain their desires, do so because theirs is weak enough to be restrained." I smooth her damp hair away from her face. William Blake would roll over in his grave, but I rather like the idea of making his sentiments my own.

I tick my chin, ordering Donavan and Micah to leave us. "I don't think this one needs the brute force."

As they exit the room, my whore arches her back, eases her hands up my thighs, seeking friction. "It's so warm…" She begins to peel her shirt up, and I catch her wrist.

"Your clothes stay on."

With a pout, she drops the hem, and is quick to move on to my thighs again.

I kick her away, and she hits the hardwood floor with a yelp. "There's a box of toys at your disposal." I nod toward the chest I had Donovan cart in. "Satisfy yourself until you're content."

51

I pull out my phone and thumb on the timer. Time to see how far my investment will go. And if my girl tires of pleasuring herself, Donovan or another can step in. Maybe a tag team approach to test the drug's stability.

I chose this specimen because she's the healthiest of the lot. All her medical tests came back clean, and of course, I exercise my girls regularly. I'm not in the business of smuggling dirty skanks; I'm in the business of providing the finest quality for my clients.

It was only logical, then, that the next step would be to rid the market of heroin-doped runts who snivel and cry. Thrash for release when they sober up. Of course, there's a particularly lucrative clientele for that market. And I have dabbled in it plenty. But my sights are set higher now. Providing the rich and powerful, the men who control the world, with willing slaves to satisfy their every desire.

Because when you control *that* market, you control the rich and powerful themselves.

As I watch her stretch her legs wide and insert a dildo into her pussy, moaning from ecstasy, the Trifecta sensitizing her nerve endings, I toggle to my contacts and locate Maddox.

"I expect everything has been arranged for tomorrow night."

There's a shuffling noise, and my agitation peaks. This should've been handled by now.

"One moment," he says.

"Take your time," I say, nudging the whore away from me

52

with my heel. She takes the hint that I'm in no mood for games and scoots farther away before proceeding to pleasure herself. "I do have others I can put in your place if this is becoming too complicated for you."

"I'm here," he says, his voice hushed. I wonder who he's trying to avoid. "But I've had some complications. There's an agent analyst here—a profiler with the ACPD—and a detective." He sighs a heavy breath. "They're asking questions and poking around, making this a difficult venture today. I thought you were going to keep the heat off me?"

My temper flares at his indignation, his assumption that I—in any way—work for him. I force my voice calm. "They'll be preoccupied soon." By now, Doctor Johnson has received my gift to her, and her team, I'm sure, is devising strategies to keep her protected.

That should keep them busy enough, giving me sufficient cover to organize the show.

"Besides," Maddox says, interrupting my thoughts. "Larkin doesn't appear to want to play by our rules."

I smile. "Just remind him of his obligation to return my favor. Or I can just as easily let him and his law firm take all the heat."

Caleb Mason—a former partner at Lark and Gannet—had a nasty habit of framing his clients for rapes he committed. When Mason decided to turn his sights on Larkin's lovely little paralegal, I took it upon myself to intervene. Mason's disappearance didn't raise any red flags for authorities—I made sure it wasn't reported. But it would've been inane on my part to dispose of Mason completely. I may just have need for him yet—at least, the easily identifiable parts of him.

"It would be ideal for Gannet to make his move to acquire the power seat of the firm," Maddox continues. "He's completely onboard."

"What is Gannet's hang-up, then?"

"Dominating share holders." A beat. "I've uncovered a failsafe in place if any of the partners attempt to procure majority of the shares. The Firm goes into a forced shutdown. Members' information is destroyed, and the members themselves disappear, as if they were never involved."

Interesting. Chase Larkin is one savvy businessman. A business model I can respect. But no system and no man is without a weakness. If he can't simply be removed as an obstacle, I'll find a way to suss out the chink in his armor.

I'm sure his pretty paralegal can help me there.

"Gannet has no theories?" I sit forward.

"There's a paralegal that Larkin seems particularly vulnerable to. I think we're devising a plan." Gannet seems to be on the same page. Good. "Otherwise, I'll have everything prepared for tomorrow night."

"I know you will." I end the call, annoyed by the tension in my neck. It's been a long time since I had to worry over an operation.

My lips tilt into a smile as I realize I'm rather enjoying the competition, though. It keeps a person sharp. And honestly, prevents boredom. Feeling frisky by this enlightenment, I stalk toward my little whore writhing on the floor.

Beads of sweat dot her face, her body slick with pent-up need. I kneel beside her and grab one of the toys. "Are you ready to perform, lovely?"

I sink my fingers into her hair and yank her head back as I drive the vibrator into her ass. She bucks at the pain, but soon she's undulating her hips with the urge to come. "Yes," she breathes.

"That's a good whore."

For the right price, we're all whores.

CHAPTER 7

ALLY

QUINN

A thick smog rolls in off the river, blotting out the afternoon sun and covering the city in a wary mood. It's an odd occurrence for this time of day. As if the atmosphere senses an impending shift.

The scent of fall in the air usually puts me at ease. It's crisp and clean, and denotes a settling for the usually chaotic flow of summer. I like it. My OCD nature relaxes against the calm.

But it's not the cleansing breeze I smell as I approach the crime scene. The hazy fog clings to my skin, stinking of rot and death. Always a fucking Dumpster. Just once, I wish a perp could be more imaginative with their dumpsites.

"Sir, you can't—" The uniform cuts his reprimand short. "Oh. Sorry, Detective Quinn." He looks uncomfortable as he rubs the back of his neck. "We were given orders not to let you—"

56

"It's all right." I wave it off. "I'm not crossing any tape." I point to the strip of yellow crime scene tape a few feet ahead of us.

He seems relieved as he nods. "Better get back at it. You wouldn't believe…" He trails off, realizing he's about to let some vital piece of information slip. He leaves before he can blunder another word.

I sigh out a painful breath from my tight lungs. The fact that Wexler hasn't lifted my suspension fucking grates. Granted, it hasn't been a full twenty-four hours yet, but I had this imagined scenario in my head that he'd come to his senses by now. It's what's kept my ego from being completely destroyed.

And seeing how Avery is invested in the case, not replying to my messages, my ego is taking a beating.

Just how needed am I?

I get the answer to that question when my phone beeps with a message. I release a tense breath. Finally.

Avery: *Sorry—been caught up. I'm okay. Everything's fine. A. King? I think I talked to them once on the forum. I thought he was another scientist. Who is he? Do you think he's one of them? Is that how they found me?*

I can feel her panic coming through the message.

Me: *You didn't do anything wrong. I'll look into it—just stay with your officer detail.*

I gaze across the taped-off crime scene. The press is stalking the scene, too, their vans stationed just feet away, reporters craning their necks to get a glimpse of the victim.

I spot Carson talking with another detective, and he looks…good. Unrattled. In control. "Nice. Real nice." The rookie is suddenly the top dog. I'm needed here about as much as a traffic cop.

When Carson notices me pacing the scene, he heads my way. "You here to get a whiff before the Feds push us out?" At my puzzled expression, he adds, "Two more bodies—" he looks around, dropping his voice "—two more were discovered, but the Feds scooped them. They've already got their team and techs at the scenes, and the precinct is crawling with black suits."

This hits me like a punch to my gut. Three bodies. In one day. Fucking hell. I weave my head, trying to locate Avery. "Same MO?" I ask. If the recent killings are tied to our case, then I can only imagine the survivor's guilt Avery is suffering right now. She escaped; those other women didn't.

I go to send her a text, but Carson says, "Hard to say. The vic's fucking skin was flayed off." I lower my phone and look up at him. "Either it's one sadistic perp," he says, "or someone wants us to think so."

Fuck. I scrub a hand down my face. "There's no way this is one offender. Depending on time of death, it would take at least two to dispose of the vics across the city." I pocket my phone and brace my hands against the back of my neck.

I need more information. TOD for all vics. Method of murder. But more than anything, I need Avery. In more ways than one.

Carson raises his eyebrows. "Gives credence to the crime ring theory."

As much as I hate to admit it, it sure as shit sounds like an organized operation. Avery was taken to design a drug for some highly organized criminals, and now it seems they're doing away with unwanted baggage.

"Might be why it's the Organized Crime Division that stepped in," Carson continues.

I drop my hands. "What?"

He looks around. "The Feds? The local Organized Crime—"

"I know that—I meant, why would they get involved?"

Carson shrugs. "They advanced the case to a serial killer, but maybe they're not buying this is the work of *one* killer. They could be thinking it's a group—an organized group—on a killing spree."

That's not bad logic. "What does Avery say?"

His face darkens, matching the sudden overcast sky. "She was pretty shaken up. The vic was dressed in a lab coat. I think it caught her off-guard."

"Where is she?"

"She went back to the crime lab to get a jump on processing trace. I'm waiting for the body pick-up crew now."

My stomach twists as I realize Avery didn't want to be around for the van to arrive. I don't fucking blame her. "Any word on the other scenes?"

Carson blows out a breath. "From what I heard, they're just as grisly as this one. Soon as the bus gets here, I'm going to push my way onto the next one. Try to get as much info as I can."

I nod. "Do me a favor," I say, slipping him a folded piece of paper. "Get this to the techs and see if they can run a search on this handle."

Before I came here, I stopped by my apartment and used Avery's laptop to track down the forum post from A_King—the screen name the kid actually came through on. There was only one short thread, but it was suspicious enough to raise my hackles. My own search didn't pull anything up; this person is well hidden in cyberworld. At least, for what my skills can detect. Finding him could mean finding the perps responsible for Avery's abduction, or at the very least, a new lead.

A King—like he's the damn king of the darknet. Pretty fucking vain handle. It's too vague to search without the proper, sophisticated tech.

"Is this something that's going to have the captain chewing my ass out?"

I narrow my gaze on Carson. "Do you care?"

He sighs. "No. Not if it means we get the bastards and Avery's safe."

My throat constricts. I'm not the only one who wants to keep her protected. I know this and yet, there's a selfish part of me that wants to be her sole protector. Her fucking hero.

"She'll need some help contacting next of kin." I look

toward the scene. "It's not easy when there's one vic, and now she has five bodies and five reports to give."

Carson nods. "I can do that. Maybe we'll get lucky and find a link among the vics. There has to be a connection."

I have a sinking feeling that these vics were chosen precisely due to their lack of connection with each other. The perp we're hunting may not be a serial killer in his own right, but his methods mimic that of one. And we can use that.

"All right. Looks like I'm out," Carson says as the transport van pulls up to the scene. "Time to see the clusterfuck the precinct has become."

"Hey—" It's right on the tip of my tongue, the words to tell him he's doing a good job. As he faces me, waiting, I drive a hand through my hair. "Keep me posted, and keep up the good work."

A slanted smile crosses his face. "Aw. Thanks, boss."

My phone beeps, breaking the awkward moment, and I'm fucking thankful. "Yeah. Just don't let the Feds get in the way."

He solutes me and heads off as I check my phone.

Sadie: *You need to get over to Lark and Gannet. Go alone.*

Me: *Rather cryptic. On my way.*

Elated. That's the only way to describe this adrenaline-charged sensation. I'm filled with purpose from one damn text. I'm halfway to my car when I realize I'm abandoning Avery for the job.

No. I'm doing the job—despite what it will cost me— *for* her. And I'm mentally arguing my point, like I need to convince my brain this is the truth. The actual truth is; I'm lost without my job.

I send Avery another message, telling her to stay put with her detail at the crime lab until I get there to pick her up. I stuff my phone away, hoping like hell she actually listens to me.

Lark and Gannet is a swanky law firm set amid the downtown courthouse district. I've been itching to get inside this building and kick up the dirt around Maddox and the other lawyers I just know have some skeletons hiding behind their doors.

And now I'm here.

It's not the way I planned—by implementing a more detective like, stealthy approach, having nailed down the dirt on them first. But we're running out of time. Avery's running out of time. I'll beat the dirt out of them if I have to.

What's the captain going to do? Suspend me?

As I walk up to the double doors, Sadie is waiting out front, her hair pulled back in a messy ponytail and her signature jean jacket open to reveal a white, nondescript T-shirt. I swear, she dresses like she's still in college just to throw suspects off their game.

It's either that, or she really doesn't want to stand out. Making herself difficult to be remembered. Trying to profile a profiler is like playing cat's cradle with my brain; once I think

I've strung a connection together, the strings get all jumbled.

I eye her curiously as I approach. "You call anything in to Wexler or the team?" I ask.

She tilts her head, squinting against the sun peeking through the clouds. "Nope. I wanted my partner's input first."

"Gee, Bonds. You really know how to stroke a guy's ego."

Her smile is sincere. "Figured you were getting bored."

That's an understatement. "What's this about?" I ask as we enter the foyer.

"Honestly, I'm not sure. Carson and I snooped around, asked some vague questions to try to get a read on the lawyers, but it wasn't until I was headed back to the department that I got a call from Chase Larkin."

I stop short and face her.

She shrugs. "He requested that we *both* meet with him. That he was adamant about. You now know as much as I do."

I seriously doubt that. Sadie has an uncanny ability to gather intel where the average person sees and hears nothing. She then has another sage ability to hide that intel away for her own future use.

I'm not knocking it…but it would be nice to channel those talents to work for us, especially now as a woman with dark hair wearing a slick business suit stalks forward. Just what are we about to get ourselves into?

"Detective Quinn and Agent Bonds?" she addresses us. Once we confirm we're in fact the ones, she directs us toward a bank of elevators. "Please, follow me."

We arrive on the top floor, where she leads us past offices and cubicles to a corner office. Chase Larkin's name printed in gold script on the door. The only door that's not glass.

"Mister Larkin is ready for you." She opens the door and leads us in.

No wait. Interesting. I don't know what I expected. When dealing with lawyers, you usually have to jump through flaming hoops and produce warrants written in blood. "You didn't have to field any evasive tactics?" I whisper to Sadie.

"Surprisingly, no. The only catch was that Larkin insisted you be here for the questioning."

I expect the woman to leave, but she takes up post next to Larkin's desk. No hidden agenda, then. We won't get anything relevant. This has to be some kind of stalling tactic.

Chase Larkin is clean shaven, slick, and probably as slippery as his silk tie. He rises from his chair and motions toward a leather sofa. "Please, make yourselves comfortable," he says. "Can I offer you anything to drink? Coffee?"

Sadie declines and I shake my head. This guy is way too welcoming and eager. Especially since he has to be aware his firm is under investigation. I nod toward a glass chessboard. "You like to play, or is the board only for decoration?"

A glib smile stretches his lips. "I enjoy a game or two on occasion."

I huff out a breath. "Well, let's try to avoid the games today." I give him my own bright smile. "I'm curious why you're so zealous to work with us, Mister Larkin. If you don't mind me

64

being blunt."

"Not at all." He walks around his desk to take a seat across from us. "This is precisely why I requested you."

A compliment, and yet he didn't answer the question. I hold my smile despite the urge to set him straight. I'm not here at *his* request. "I think you want us to see how cooperative you and your firm are, prove just how little you have to hide. I hope you're not wasting our time, because I'm sure you're aware by now of the murders plaguing our city."

His sharp features darken. "Detective Quinn, I'm very aware of that, and the fact that, technically, you have no right to be questioning me at all. Considering you've been suspended." He laces his hands together atop his desk. "But I like your no-bullshit manner. And I think we can help each other."

Sadie cuts her eyes at me, and I know—the only reason Larkin wants me here is simple: anything he divulges can be thrown out due to my suspension. Fucking lawyers.

I nod for her to address Larkin. "A partner at your firm was acquainted with one of the victims," she says. "Do you have any knowledge of Marcy Beloff? Or how Ryland Maddox was associated with her?"

Larkin relaxes back in his chair. "I think you're asking the wrong questions. You're going about this like a simple murder investigation."

She cranes an eyebrow. "And just how should we be conducting this interview?"

He looks at the woman. "Alexis, can you please give the

officers the copies." The woman, Alexis, does as instructed, quickly gathering papers off his desk. "Miss Wilde will now show you something that I trust will remain between us; it can't leave this office. For obvious reasons, my name can't be implicated in your investigation. Any information I give you must be of a confidential source." He holds up a hand, and Miss Wilde halts her steps. "I need to be assured of this before any information is exchanged."

If I ever shook hands with the devil, I have a feeling he'd be wearing an Armani suit and silk tie. Sadie lays her hand near me on the couch, signaling that she's ready to try to restrain me if needed. She knows I'm about two seconds away from jacking this guy up by his collar and shaking the information out of him.

If he has anything, *anything* at all that will help Avery, he's giving it to me before I leave this room. How ever I have to obtain it.

Regardless, for the sake of his game, I'll give him the illusion he's in control. I suck down a tight breath. "I assure you, Mister Larkin, whatever transpires in this room will not leave." And it better be damn good.

His smile isn't as smug as it should be. He nods once, giving Miss Wilde permission to advance. "Mister Larkin received this message the day he was visited by an anonymous man," she says.

She first hands Sadie a photocopied page, and then one to me. My eyebrows pull together as I stare at a copy of a business card, front and back. The card belongs to Ryland Maddox, attorney at law. His number and firm address, but it's the backside of the card that sets my jaw.

It's just a signature, but one I now recognize as the Alpha.

"Where's the original?" I ask.

"Someplace safe."

"You're trying to tell us the Alpha gave you Maddox's business card?" I look Larkin right in the eyes. "Why? Is he the Alpha?"

He holds my stare. "I'm not trying to tell you anything, Detective Quinn. I'm imparting sensitive information to you. Information on the very criminal network you're investigating. And I don't know whether Maddox is the Alpha or not."

I shake my head, set the paper aside. "Giving us a false lead to take the heat off of your firm isn't only tactless, it's illegal. As I'm sure you know, I can charge you with interference."

"I can assure you," Alexis says, turning all heads her way. "We're very aware of the implication of falsifying evidence. I'm a witness to the transaction that took place between Mister Larkin and the anonymous source."

I shift my gaze to Larkin, studying him. "Maybe you should let your assistant head this up," I say. "Miss Wilde seems a little more prepared to tango with the ACPD."

Sadie sits forward. I can tell she's losing patience with my temper. "Let's assume this message is real. Why you, Mister Larkin? Why would the head of a criminal network direct you to hire a specific lawyer?"

Larkin sits forward, elbows to knees, and steeples his fingers together. "So they can have access to The Firm."

I shake my head. "That's too vague. You know what this person wants from you. Specifically. Money laundering? Or something more appealing. Like representing members of this crime ring. Making sure they don't see a day of prison." I narrow my gaze on him. "Just like your boy Maddox already appears to be doing."

His features harden. I struck a nerve. He's the boss here. The man in control. And seeing how he not only hired Maddox but made him an equal partner, he submitted to this request. Which means, whoever gave him this card has some pretty big dirt on Larkin.

"You're thinking too small, detective." Larkin stands and leans against his desk, making sure he's looking down at us. "This person doesn't just want access to my law firm—they want access to *The* Firm." At my obvious confusion, he says, "I run an exclusive members only organization for the..." He pauses here, selecting his words carefully. "For the elites of society. Those who wish not to have their sexual appetites exposed to the world."

Fucking hell. This city is crawling with fucking perverts. I spear a hand through my hair, purposely avoiding eye contact with Sadie. This is right up her alley, and I suddenly feel bitter. Bitter and angry—angry that I have no knowledge of the underground workings of my own city.

Naivety is the worst disposition. I'm like a giant, goofy kid stumbling around in the sandbox with the rest of the cool kids.

Despite my desire to shred this topic and get immediate answers, I let Sadie take the lead on this one. It's her damn area of expertise, and I need to pay attention to any subtle nuances during their exchange.

Picking up on my cue, Sadie proceeds, looking far less disturbed by this information than me. "So The Firm belongs to you," she says, and I want to balk. Of course she knows of its existence. Her and Rope Boy probably frequent it.

Larkin smiles, impressed. "Actually, it belongs to the members. I just oversee it. Make sure everybody plays by the rules."

She nods slowly. "Rules are very important to you," she continues as she stands and walks to the glass chessboard. "You've constructed your life, and your company, around certain rules you deem essential, and a threat to that structure would be quite a stressor."

Sadie touches a piece on the board, looks over her shoulder at Larkin. Some tentative battle of wills arcs between them. I can see it in the way Larkin's lips thin. His gaze steady on the chess piece. A pawn.

Finally, Larkin meets Sadie's eyes and smiles. "I'm not one of your subjects to analyze. You can profile me all you want, but you're wasting your time. That won't get you any closer to your goal, Agent Bonds."

Sadie slides the pawn forward on the board and then faces Larkin. "And we're not going to become pawns in your game,

Mister Larkin. If the Alpha is a threat to you, you'd simply have him eliminated. Game over. But you've welcomed us in to do your dirty work." She crosses her arms and moves closer to his desk. "Either you know who the Alpha is and you realize that you, yourself, can't touch him. Or you don't know his identity at all, and you want us to flush him out for you."

Larkin's smile is brilliant and practiced. "Touché, agent. You are quite good."

Sadie cocks her head. "So which is it, and how do you plan to slither away from this unscathed?"

He straightens his back. All facade erased from his serious demeanor. "Ferreting out the Alpha serves to help me as much as it does you." He inclines his head, letting us know Sadie was right in her deduction. "Why else would I suggest it if it didn't benefit me? Every single person on this planet is self-involved. We all orchestrate games and have agendas to benefit ourselves."

"All right." I jump in. "I'm tired of being on this merry-go-round. Do you have anything useful for us, or is this just a ruse to garner information for yourself? I'm one minute away from having my partner take you in for impeding our investigation."

He shoots me a glare. Doesn't like being threatened; Sadie nailed that one dead-on. "What if I told you I might have knowledge as to where the Alpha will be tomorrow night?"

This forces me off the sofa. I approach him with locked fists. "I'd say you have less than a minute now."

Sadie touches my arm, and I stop. But if whatever he

does know can remove Avery as a target…then I'll get that information. One way or another.

Larkin shares a look with Alexis, and she nods, encouraging him. I don't understand the dynamic between him and his assistant, but I'm mentally storing her sway over him for later use.

"I do know where the Alpha will be tomorrow night," Larkin says, squaring his shoulders. "We have one small window of opportunity for all of us to get what we want. And we *will* do it my way—" he glances between Sadie and me "—because I won't have the FBI or your clumsy task force fucking it up."

It's the first bit of true backbone I've seen from Larkin so far. Smug fucker. I smile. I can work with that.

CHAPTER 8

RABBIT HOLE

AVERY

*T*he crime lab has become something akin to Alcatraz. Chief security measures have been enforced, assuring that no one outside the lab techs and law enforcement gain entry. Officers stand guard at the entrance, requiring all technicians and interns to sign in, then they're checked against the databases.

Not just safeguarding; this lab is under surveillance.

This level of invasiveness is more than unnerving. I feel trapped. Like a rat spinning a wheel, round and round, just waiting for one of my monitors to toss in a stick to trip me up. And then the whole charade comes crashing down.

Honestly, I'm almost relieved it could be over. Exhaustion has started to toy with my mind. Paranoia has crept into my work. I question every look, every statement from my techs. I'm slipping.

And granted, even though the added security ensures the safety of my lab, it also affects my staff. Since the occurrence yesterday... No, scratch that. Since the first time I was taken by Wells, there's been a lingering thread of fear running through this place.

Although everyone is too considerate to call it out for what it is, it's there. Hovering just below their forced, kind smiles. They either hate the censoring as much as I do, or they want out, transferred altogether.

They were working alongside a sadistic killer for months...I can't fault them for wanting to get far away from this madhouse.

Besides, with the FBI introducing—not too subtly—their special medical examiner team, we've been sidelined. We've become *their* helpers. I'm not sure why I was even called to the first crime scene today other than they wanted to test me. Analyze my reaction to the vic draped in my lab coat.

Or that could just be my paranoia.

The lab coat has been identified as mine now. Special forensic medical examiner in charge, Aubrey Paulsen, pointed it out only moments ago. He then proceeded to admonish me in front of my own lab, requesting in a not-so-requesting manner for me to take the rest of the evening off.

I'm not going anywhere until the other two victims are brought in. I have to know if there's another warning against me on their person. I have to know if this will all circle back to me, and my role in the disposal of Wells.

The masked man knew what I'd done, and he threatened to make it known. By escaping and thwarting his plans—whatever horrible fate he had intended for me—I've set this in motion.

How will he reveal my secret?

I press my palms against the autopsy cart. The cool steel helps stabilize my breathing. The truth is, I set this in motion the moment I looked Sadie in the eyes and wished for my captor's death. Once it became reality, there was no turning back. This warped and ugly reality is my reward, and once the world knows, I won't fear for my life anymore.

Is physical death less of a punishment than the death of my career and reputation? I feel disgusting for comparing such a thing.

Death or prison? I'd rather not have to choose between either.

The double doors swing open with a loud *bang* and I flinch. My black thoughts are pushed aside as I prepare myself. I dust my hands off on my coat as the transfer crew wheel the body toward the center of the lab.

Doctor Paulsen rests his hand on my shoulder, and I nearly leap away from his touch. "Relax," he says, but removes his hand. "I'm just going to reiterate my thoughts about you taking the night off, Doctor Johnson." His light gray eyes and strikingly handsome features turn down in consideration. "You don't have to be here for this."

My defenses flare. I should be here for this, as this is my lab. "I appreciate your concern, Doctor Paulsen." I pull a pair of gloves from my pocket. "But I'm sure you'd want to be present in your own lab in such a circumstance."

His lips twist into a slight smile. "Of course. And please, you can call me Aubrey. No formalities among colleagues, all right?"

I free a strained breath, accepting with a nod. "Avery is fine, also. Thank you."

The momentary camaraderie is soon dispelled when the second body arrives, completing today's body count at three. Aubrey does the honors and signs off on the delivery while I take measured steps toward the second victim.

After completing my examination of the first, documenting the brutality she suffered, I feel I'm prepared to face this next challenge. I'm not, however, prepared for the thick bile that burns my throat at the noxious smell.

I unzip the white body bag and suppress a gasp.

She's been disemboweled.

This victim still has her skin—but her insides have been eviscerated. Her sternum sliced open, right through her chest cavity down to her pelvis. Split down the middle like a sunbaked, overripe watermelon.

How long did she remain alive through the torture?

I look away, hating that I'll soon discover the answer to that question.

Aubrey begins recording the vic's stats, moving right

75

along to the grotesque facts of her death. I listen while he details every removed organ, and lists the few remains of her intestines and entrails that spill over her stomach wall.

"Flora Porter was twenty years of age and—"

"What?"

His gaze flicks to me, his examination interrupted. With a *click*, he stops the recorder. "Is there an issue, Avery?"

Yes, there's a damn issue. "How do you know her name already?"

His mouth purses into a thin line, his shoulders deflate. "The FBI have a rather rapid response to victim identification. I believe one of your officers has already been dispatched to contact the victim's next of kin."

I inhale a stale breath. "And the others?" Where were the FBI and their extensive, state-of-the-art databases when I was weeding through searches on the very first victim? If we'd had that information before I was taken… No. I can't go there. Nothing would've stopped Mister AK Tie from getting what he wanted. The drug. This all comes back to the drug, and God—there's an FBI medical examiner in my lab, surrounded by evidence of the drug, who will soon link all the connections.

Quinn. I need you.

And it hits me then. Connection. *The* connection. The initials AK on the crest of the necktie…A. King. The forum poster.

I can't blame this oversight on exhaustion; I refused to see it. My darknet searches for ambergris did lead them to me—it

76

is my fault. And then, somehow, this man unearthed my evil secret to use against me—to guarantee my cooperation.

"Avery?"

I snap myself out of my thoughts. I can't do this here. I have to hold it together. "And the other victims?" I ask, concealing the tremble in my voice.

"I believe we're on track with them, as well." He grabs his tablet and swipes the screen. "Vita Laurent and Sidra Girard have both been identified. Laurent was reported missing by her parents in Prague, but Girard was 'chalked up' as a runaway. Girard's family is still trying to be located."

I glance around the lab, noticing eyes watching me, bodies stilled in anticipation for my reaction. Natalie clears her throat and resumes her data entry on the trace at the first scene, and the rest follow suit. The room reboots with its usual hum of activity.

Aubrey ticks his head toward my office, silently requesting that we handle this out of earshot. I don't hide from my coworkers, though. Since the abduction, my life has become an open book.

"They're foreign," I say, keeping the escalating panic from creeping into my tone.

With a deliberate nod, Aubrey says, "Yes. From what we've garnered, all the victims were originally from outside the US." He toggles his screen. "Marcy Beloff was initially from Canada before she took up residence in Arlington. She's the only local victim, however."

My mind is spinning theories. Everything coming at me at supersonic speed. A dizzying rush attacks my equilibrium. I grip the edge of the table.

"Avery. I'm sorry, but I don't understand." Aubrey approaches me with caution. "We're not detectives or agents. Our job isn't to speculate or connect evidence with theories. We're just gathering the facts."

For a medical examiner who doesn't read into theories, he's deducing one about me pretty well right now. "I understand this. But I was also very nearly a victim myself." I head around the cart toward the last victim. "So excuse me if this case is a bit more personal for me."

His sigh is audible over the lab clamor. "And that's exactly why I suggested you take time off."

That stings. I whirl around, the end of my ponytail slaps my cheek. "Which doesn't conclude that I can't be objective and do my job."

I'm not a confrontational person by nature. I don't seek out conflict, and I really don't want to go toe-to-toe with some FBI medical examiner. But I've been abducted, drugged, and damn near killed in the past forty-eight hours, and amid it all, I've had my lab infiltrated.

The one place that I used to feel the most myself in will never, *ever* be mine again.

"We need to determine the cause of death for this vic," I say, directing his exasperated attention to the final cadaver. Once I have conclusive findings to all their deaths, I might actually have a worthy update for Quinn.

I peel away the body bag to examine the last victim. Her toe tag does in fact list her name. She didn't go easily. She put up a vicious fight. Good for her.

Her frail body is covered in lacerations and contusions. Defensive wounds cover her arms and legs. At least she has limbs…and skin and viscera.

"With each vic, the perp stepped up the method of torture," I say, thinking out loud. "What happened to you?" I whisper to the victim.

Aubrey shakes his head, and I glance up. "What?" I ask.

"You must work closely with the detectives in your building." He adjusts his gloves as he takes up a place opposite the victim. "You sound just like them."

A small smile tugs at my lips. "We are a pretty close unit." Heat splashes the back of my neck at the memory of Quinn in my kitchen.

"See this here?" He points to a dark ring of bruises around her neck, and I refocus my thoughts. "It appears the victim was strangled as the…perp"—he glances up—"submerged her."

I find how he came to the drowning conclusion right away. Her skin is bloated, but not of a normal degree due to typical death bloat, and the petechial hemorrhaging, the blood dotting her pale eyes, isn't pooled at the bottom of her lids, like it would be if it settled there naturally at her death. The offender could've submerged her right after she was asphyxiated, the broken vessels of her eyes bleeding out into the water, but I believe we'll discover water in her lungs to constitute she was drowned.

"We should open the vic up to confirm." I turn toward my tray of tools.

"From the degree and number of contusions along her neck, and the varying placements…" He pauses as he pulls back the bag shielding her torso. "Yes, she has bruising on her chest, too." He presses his fingers along her rib cage and applies pressure. "At least two broken ribs."

I feel the blood drain from my face, cold and prickling in its wake. "He resuscitated her."

His gaze meets mine, his mouth curved in a hard frown. "Many times. To drown her all over again."

My eyes are drawn to the other victims, their gory demise, their brutal torture. Their suffering was excruciating. And yet, they only had to endure it once. As I look at the last victim again, her skin pale and drained of life, her unseeing eyes dull, I break down.

My bones are liquid by the time the last COD report is submitted. My muscles burn, my shoulder that was wrenched during my struggle in the lab yesterday throbs, the pain medication having worn off hours ago.

Aubrey insisted on staying after I let my techs go for the evening. They've seen me nearly broken before, but my breakdown earlier was shocking even for me. I'm too drained to be embarrassed. The fragile walls I've erected could come tumbling down any second.

All Aubrey has to do is ask the right questions—about the drug, about the men who abducted me. In a moment of sheer exhaustion, I'd confess everything.

He doesn't ask, though. He records facts and findings, and doesn't entertain theories. I do admire his work ethic and skills, but I couldn't answer to the FBI the way he does. There's an almost military structure and code that makes me claustrophobic just being near him.

As I massage my shoulder, working out the ache, my phone vibrates in my pocket. I pull it out and look down, my heart unsure whether it wants to stop beating or rejoice.

Quinn: *I'm parked out front.*

I hadn't actually thought about what would happen once I left the lab. This morning where Quinn, rather domineeringly, insisted I stay with him feels like ages ago. So much has transpired since then.

I wonder why he hasn't just come into the lab like he usually does, until I recall the security officers guarding the entrance. I hurriedly reply that I'm on my way out.

In my office, I tuck the flash drive where I saved my reports on the victims into my pocket, then lock up. I awkwardly wave to Aubrey as I head toward the double doors. There's suddenly a pull in my belly, some string tethered within my body, drawing me in Quinn's direction as if by aberrant force.

I've successfully avoided him all day, even though I promised to keep him updated. I just…couldn't. I couldn't pretend to be on top of this job while everything inside me was fighting to keep breathing through the suffocating madness of it all.

Quinn's demanding, authoritative nature reminds me too much of the scientist I used to be. Besides, from the moment I saw the tortured victim, and realized these girls are dying because of me…

I knew my secret is no longer mine to keep.

It's time.

I just wanted to postpone the inevitable as long as I could. Savor the comforting feeling I get when I think of Quinn's hands on me. His mouth caressing, lingering. Because once he knows the truth, those moments between us will evaporate into oblivion as if they never existed.

As I nod to the officer stationed outside the main door, I spot Quinn leaning against his dented car. And Sadie on the other side.

Immediately, a vise-like grip clutches my airway, and the cool, evening air makes me shiver. There's a hint of dead leaves in the air despite there being no trees in the parking lot. It's the kind of foreboding you sense coming in a movie, when the main character is creeping toward an unavoidable, doomed outcome.

I walk steadily toward them, aware that I'm the idiot girl in my own movie, heading straight for a cataclysmic end. My only hope is that I'll be able to repair the damage from the fallout between Quinn and I in the sequel.

Either way, I'm exhausted from secrets. I know Sadie will try to stop me, talk me out of it, for my own good…but I'm ready to face my consequences and do whatever I have to in order to stop the evil that has descended over all of us with these murders. If Quinn can suss out just one clue from my horror story with Wells, if there's any connection at all to him and these villainous men, then it's worth my freedom.

Sadie must see the determination in my eyes, and she's quick to be the first to approach me. "We have a plan," she says, her unearthly green eyes pleading with me to be patient. "Come on. Let's get you somewhere you can rest."

An unspoken exchange passes between us, where she encourages me to trust her just a while longer. I exhale a plume of vapor into the cool air, my constricted chest too tight. "What plan?"

Quinn drives a hand through his tousled hair, looking like he's done just that a number of times already today. "There's no fucking plan," he grates out. "But I agree with getting you home."

Our gazes lock. All the worry and weight of the longing moments between us stretched thin, ready to snap. He reaches for my hand, and I only hesitate a second before grabbing hold of him. His rough fingers wrap around my slim ones in a secure squeeze.

Sadie motions for me to take the front seat, then she slips

83

into the back, where I notice Colton for the first time. My shock must register with Quinn.

"Oh, yeah. There's a plan all right," he says, directing his words toward the backseat. "One where I drop the both of you off at whatever raunchy establishment you want."

A flash of anger flints in Colton's pale eyes. "Believe me," he says as he slides Sadie closer to his side. "I'm no fan of anything that has me sitting in the back of your cop car."

I buckle myself in and turn toward Quinn. "What plan?" I ask again.

He shakes his head and cranks the car. "The one that will have every single one of us put on a list with the FBI, never mind losing all our jobs, risking imprisonment for obstruction..." He glances at me. "You ever heard of The Firm?"

I shake my head.

The tension gripping his body immediately slackens. "I can't stress enough how fucking happy that makes me."

CHAPTER 9

SEDITION

QUINN

I pull into the parking space alongside Carson's car and throw the gear into Park with an impatient groan. "Who called Carson?"

"We're going to need backup," Sadie says, and my teeth clench.

I don't like it. Not one fucking bit. It's too...Sadie. The whole thing stinks of her methods and tactics, and it's way out of my comfort zone. Too much can go wrong. Someone can get hurt. *Avery* could get hurt.

My gaze wanders to her sitting calmly in the passenger-seat. She looks exhausted. She's already been through so much. When Larkin suggested using her in his scheme, that's the second I walked out.

He's damn lucky I didn't put my fist through his face first.

I scrub my hands down my face, feeling every bit as worn

out as this day. "All right. Let's get this over with." The sooner I can veto this idiotic plan, the sooner I can convince Avery to sleep. Something we both need.

For a brief second as I insert my key into the door lock, a niggle of anxiety tenses my shoulders. I never have people at my house. Ever. I'm rarely even here, except to sleep and shower. And as I lead my colleagues into the living area, that's pretty damn obvious.

Blank walls and sparse decoration. Books and research stacked high on the only table in the center, a small flatscreen hung on the wall. Even though it's not much, it's still my personal space, and having them here feels like an invasion of privacy.

"Wow. Where the great Detective Quinn lays his head," Carson remarks. "Can the profiler give us any interesting insights into the man?" He thrusts his hands into his pockets and rocks back on his heels, sending Sadie a self-satisfied look.

Sadie smiles, something as rare as company inside my home, and the room warms just because of it. "You mean the fact that he's a complete neat freak with OCD tendencies, and instead of chancing a mess, he simply avoids personal possessions?"

Avery lilts a tiny laugh, and the scowl on my face melts away. "Funny, smartasses." I scoop the books off the table and set them on the bookshelf, then think better and align them in order next to the other books along the row.

Sadie's snort doesn't go unnoticed. "Yeah, all right," I say.

"I like my shit tidy. Can we just move this along past mock-Quinn-hour?"

Carson clears his throat. "Right, boss. So what is this big clandestine plan we're keeping from the Feds and the captain? From what Agent Bonds said, seems we got a lead from that lawyer—Larkin."

A lead. More like a setup. Larkin was quick to confirm my suspicions on Maddox. Rather too quick, considering he's throwing one of his own right under a giant bus. The way I see it, he wants Maddox out of his firm, but because he's being extorted, he can't do that himself. He's trying to orchestrate a means to rid himself of his blackmailer without getting his own hands dirty.

I give him credit; he's thought it through, and knows we're inclined not to involve the Feds. I'm not opposed to this whole plan in general, not if it means collaring the suspects and getting Avery out of danger. But crime is crime. Right is right, and wrong is wrong. Whatever Larkin is guilty of, whatever got him mixed up with these criminals to begin with, isn't just going to disappear off my radar.

Larkin has to be aware of this fact. Aware that once we do make an arrest, one of the perps is bound to turn on Larkin. Either to plea for a deal, or just out of spite.

How does Larkin think he's going to play this game and come out clean on the other side? Or alive, for that matter.

Only when I sneak a glance at Avery, take in her sullen lethargy, and remember the pain on her face this morning

87

when it was crystal fucking clear she *was* hurt by this so called Alpha...all logic vanishes.

How far will I go down this dark path to protect her?

Sadie picks up on Carson's prompt, interrupting my disturbed thoughts. "We've made a deal."

"No deal," I say, cutting my eyes at her. "We don't make deals with miscreants."

At Sadie's exasperated sigh, Avery chimes in. "It didn't sound to me like he's a miscreant...I mean, yes, he operates a kinky BDSM club, but that's not illegal, is it?"

All heads turn toward Colton, that question unmistakably directed at him.

Arms crossed, his back leaned up against the wall, he shrugs. Fucking smug bastard. "He's not doing anything illegal," he finally answers. "He's offering a service to people who don't want their fetishes broadcasted. Some people might not be open-minded enough to accept it." His gaze skirts the room to narrow on me.

I almost laugh. "Accept it? It's kind of hard to accept when your rope fetish—"

"Shibari," he interjects.

"—looks a lot like crime scene photos of a sadistic perp's bondage fantasy," I finish.

"Can someone just tell me what the hell this is all about?" Carson asks.

"Trafficking."

It's Avery's gentle voice that slices through the tension.

"Sex Trafficking," she clarifies as she looks around the room. "Abducting women in other countries and making them disappear. Bringing them here to sell to the highest bidder. Dosing them with a highly effective aphrodisiac that will not only make them compliant, tolerant of their hopeless circumstance, but the most sought after sex slaves money can buy."

Silence falls heavy and thick. Each person contemplative, allowing this information to sink in. But I have to know—the detective in me needs all the facts. "How do you know this?"

The slim column of Avery's throat bobs. She reaches into her pocket and produces a USB drive. "The FBI medical examiner identified the victims. All foreign. Most have an open missing person's case in their country." She lays the drive on the table. "It's all documented here."

That's a logical leap to trafficking. Factor in the drug, and these perps have a very lucrative business. A fucking sick business—but one that's becoming the fastest growing criminal enterprise in the world.

My gaze lingers on Avery, on the nervous tremble of her body. She may be exhausted, but there's something else she's not voicing. I can see it in her downcast eyes. The way she tugs at her lip.

"The Feds have taken over contacting the families?" I ask.

She forces her hand to her lap and looks up. "Yes. As long as the case is open here, we can retain the victims for further examination. But I'm sure they're going to want to lay them to rest—I mean, I'm sure we'll have to extradite them soon."

She can fool herself all she wants, hardening herself into a top professional of her field, but I glimpse the mournful compassion beneath her well constructed doctor persona.

"And Chase Larkin provided proof to back Avery's discovery today," Sadie interjects. She looks at Colton and holds his gaze, as if gathering courage. "The person who calls themself the Alpha is conducting an underground auction tomorrow night at The Firm. Larkin's exclusive association."

She doesn't have to voice what the merchandise is. If it's true, if the murdered women that have been appearing near Dumpsters have only been a diversion for this auction, then we're facing a special brand of evil.

"Why there?" Carson asks. "I mean, why would the Alpha trust a venue that's not specifically his to control. Why run the risk?"

Good question, rook. I go to respond, but my front door rattles with a low knock before it's opened. I reach for my gun and curse. But Sadie and Carson are quick to draw theirs.

"Resources." Larkin stands in the threshold, then seeing the weapons, squares his shoulders. "And here I thought we were invited."

As Sadie and Carson lower their guns, I take off toward Larkin. "Rich lawyers suddenly supersede breaking and entering laws?" I march past him and check the outside corridor.

Alexis smiles demurely at me as she crosses into the

apartment behind Larkin. Once I clear the corridor, making sure Larkin doesn't have any uninvited guests loitering, I shut and *lock* the door.

"In retrospect, I probably should've waited," Larkin says, that annoying, million-watt lawyer smile on full display. "Definitely don't want to get *shot*. However, I thought it would be ideal to get out of eyesight as soon as possible."

Risking a lot, or not worth the risk? His whole agenda is shady, and his presence sucks the meager light right out of the room. His other half—Alexis—stands beside him, her hands cupped before her black pencil skirt, his dark little shadow.

"Well, let's not chance being seen together any longer than necessary," I say, crossing my arms. "Give me one reason why I shouldn't just hand you over to the Feds."

It's Alexis who steps forward to answer. "Because they're tainted."

My brows push together. "What do you mean?"

"As I was saying," Larkin stresses. "My firm has resources. Superlative resources. The Alpha has targeted my firm because they want all potential buyers vetted beforehand." He mirrors my stance, gaze unwavering. "And due to those resources, I've been made aware of a possible breach in the local FBI Organized Crime Division. That's why I didn't reach out to them."

"What breach?"

He glances around my living room, quickly assessing everyone here. "You know how likely it is to have a leak within your department, Detective Quinn. The FBI aren't without their own security challenges."

Right. If it smells like bullshit… "That aside, you think we're your best option to rid you of your problem." I lift my chin.

"Exactly." He smiles. "As I said before, we can both get what we desire by working together."

I shake my head. "What makes you think you have any idea—?"

"You want Miss Johnson safe." His attention shifts to Avery. "From how you've all gathered here, potentially risking your careers, you all want the same."

A pang knocks my chest. No one responds, because it's damn true.

I take a step forward. "Since you're so perceptive, tell me how the fuck you can ask any one of us to allow Avery into The Firm."

Yet Avery's the one to stand and answer. "I can't and *won't* risk anyone else. I'm willing to be the one to do this." She takes a breath. "I should be the one."

"She'll be protected there," Alexis assures. She glances at Avery. "I'll be there with her, and I promise she won't be harmed. She'll be more protected there than anywhere else in this city. No one has reason to suspect her of being there."

My jaw sets at hearing this woman use Avery's name. I find Avery's eyes, seeking her answer. For whatever reason, whether it's her own selfless nature or the drive to be noble, or

WITH TIES THAT BIND: Broken Bonds, Book Two

the need to see her job through to this impossible end… She's determined to do it.

Sadie speaks up. "Quinn, if I could, I would take her place. You know I would." She lowers the collar of her shirt, revealing the thick scar marring her collarbone. "But, no amount of cosmetics will hide my identity."

What's not being voiced: How any of the members or lawyers at The Firm would know her identity. But they do, and not just due to Larkin's "extensive resources." Sadie has some other connection to this law firm and, I swear, before this is all said and done, I'll have answers.

"We'll dye your hair," Alexis says to Avery. "And, of course, a little cosmetics will help conceal your scar." She smiles wanly as Avery touches her lip. "But more than that, you'll be required to wear a mask. I'll make sure it's one to hide your features well."

Fuck this. I don't like it. Hell, I downright loathe the idea of Avery going anywhere near those sick fuckers. But… "I'm going in with her."

"You can't."

I pin Larkin with a heated glare. "If she goes in, I go in with her."

"You chased down a transport van in broad daylight and beat the shit out of one of the suspects, Detective Quinn. These people know who you are." He looks at Carson. "You're detective here, however, well—he would work."

I drop my head, a defeated laugh falling from my mouth

before I'm able to look up again. "And how's that?"

Larkin's smile sets me on edge. "He's your leak," he says simply. "He already has a well known reputation in the gambling ring. He's not our ideal member, of course, but with a little tweaking, his background could be forged to better suit one of a potential buyer at the auction."

Silence builds, squeezing the room in a tense grip. My gaze hard and steady, unable to move past Larkin, I say slow and concise, "What did you say?"

With a huff, Larkin fixes his eyes on Carson. "Superlative resources, detective. Alec Carson has been feeding information to the press for a price to help pay off his gambling debt."

His words aren't registering clearly, his voice an annoying background noise to the blood cooking my veins, rushing past my ears. When I manage to look at Carson, the roar of blood crescendos. Carson doesn't deny it.

"You fucking piece of shit—" I'm across the room and have Carson by his collar and against the wall in three steps.

"Quinn…let me explain." He latches on to my wrists, tries to remove my hold. I curl my fingers in deeper as I snap his back against the wall hard.

"You fucking sold out your own department?"

"Just a few times." He actually says this, sending rage careening through my arteries. "Not when it mattered."

"Quinn—" Sadie's voice bleeds into my awareness. "Stop. This is good."

My gaze swings to her, my eyes wide. Of course she has no

qualms about Carson being a greedy leak. Forcefully relaxing my hold, I loosen my fingers just enough for Carson to wriggle free.

I scan the room, darting glances at each person in my house. People hide things. About themselves, their personal lives—problems and how they cope with their issues. I'm not fucking heartless; I get that some extremes are a necessary evil. But being a leak is pretty low on my list.

Sadie's secrets, her double life has nearly cost her and others—me included—more than our careers. Lives were at stake.

When my gaze lands on Avery, I feel as if I've been sucker punched right in the gut. Fear is evident on her pretty face—fear of me. My fists still locked by my sides, arms trembling with strain, I hate myself for questioning her. Trying to read her. Figure out if she's fearful of me…or if she's hiding her own secrets.

I shake myself out of that thought and turn back toward Carson, who's still pressed up against the wall and eyeing me like I might attack him again.

He holds up his hands. "It really was just a few times. I was just…desperate. But when Avery was abducted—" He swallows. "I quit. I promise."

"He's telling the truth," Larkin says.

My fury is directed toward him and his interference with my team, my investigation, and now my life. "This ends now."

"Please," Avery says. "Let's just hear him out, then we'll all decide."

I wave my hand through the air. "Why do I care when Carson stopped leaking like a damn faucet?"

"Because it's important to your investigation." Larkin moves toward the center of the room. "I was the one who leaked the Alpha's signature to the media."

And inadvertently or not, may have caused the death of three women. Sickened, I shake my head. "I've heard enough. You should've contacted me before making such a fucking dumb move, Larkin." I grab the USB drive from the table and head toward my bedroom. "Everyone can see themselves out."

Avery grabs my arm as I try to pass, halting me. "I have to do this, Quinn."

The pain in her voice stabs my chest. "We'll discuss it later. I put your stuff in the guest bedroom."

She releases me, taking a step away. "Fine. All right."

I shut the door behind me, escaping into my room where I might be able to hear my own thoughts. Only the low rumble of voices coming from the main room steals that sanctuary.

It comes down to this—this moment. This choice. A lifetime of devotion to my work and morals and beliefs, all summed up to a broken man without a badge.

Divorced. No kids. Ulcer the size of a planet. Surrounded by colleagues who may or may not be as corrupt as the criminals I've sacrificed everything to hunt.

And now, wallowing in self-pity. I suppress a humorless laugh.

I drag myself over to the bed and flop down, rest my arm over my eyes. When I held Avery's hand in the hospital all those nights, I vowed to protect her. Not because it was my job—because I saw the light I'd come to depend on from her snuffed out. No one has the right to take that away.

But they did. She's changed because of that torment, and I'm not sure if any damn thing I do will ever bring it back.

I don't fall asleep. I can't. I lie here with a torrent of thoughts thrashing my brain until I hear the front door latch closed. But my muscles don't relax until I hear the gentle rap on my bedroom door.

CHAPTER 10

BARE

AVERY

'm not searching for love. That's never been a desire of mine. I didn't turn down every date and party invite in high school, sit home every weekend with my nose crammed in a book throughout college, just to throw away all that hard work now on a fantasy dreamed up by some desperate part of myself.

Yeah. That was a little harsh. Even for me. But I'm furious for allowing myself to fantasize about a future I can never have—not with the man behind this door.

So this thing with Quinn…I know it's temporary. I might even be using him as a distraction from all the horror that's sucked my life up into a dark cyclone of pain and cruelty.

And when I admit that—that my feelings for Quinn might only be as deep as this case, there's only one outcome: Quinn will suffer the agony of my choices.

He's already been suspended. His wife left him. His partner is a serial killer.

He's discovering every person in his life isn't what they seem. Especially me.

Despite it all, regardless if I *should* walk away, I'm selfish and crave just one more moment of comfort his touch brings.

It's impossible to deny I'm falling in love.

Maybe for the first time.

It might be layering additional cruelty onto his burdens, but waiting any longer will only inflict more torture than I can bear for him. So I knock again, harder, and this time, the door opens.

He's loosened his tie; it hangs open around his neck, his crisp white dress shirt unbuttoned at the top and rumpled from where he untucked it from his slacks. He might feel like a mess, but as he stands in the doorway, arm braced high on the door, he's the steadfast strength I've anchored myself to.

"Can I come in?"

Without a word, he pulls the door open wider.

One dimly lit lamp welcomes me into the room as I enter. Quinn's scent surrounds me; masculine and heady, like the metal headboard and clean angles of his room. I stare at the bed. A gray comforter is pulled tight across the mattress. Pillows lined neatly along the head.

I'm probably the filthiest thing to ever enter his room. I'm spoiling it just by standing here. I tuck my hands under my arms so I don't mar anything with my touch.

"You should rest." He nods to the pristinely made bed. "At least lay down for a while."

I stay put. "I'm sorry about Carson."

His sigh is heavy as he settles on the edge of the bed. Runs a hand through his hair. "It's not that big of a deal."

But for him, I know it is. Quinn's ethics are important, and Carson let him down. We're all letting him down. I risk a step closer. "I'm tired, Quinn."

He looks up. "Then sleep, Avery."

I shake my head. "I'm tired of lying to you."

There's no hint in his frozen expression that I've shaken him. He doesn't blink. Those hazel eyes darken just a shade and spear me, stripping me bare where I stand.

Maybe it's exhaustion, why I suddenly feel so removed from this reality and like I've entered into an alternate one where, once I admit the truth, Quinn wraps those strong arms around me and accepts my sins...because when I say it, and the floodgates are unlatched, the confession rushes from me unfiltered.

"Simon wasn't the UNSUB. He wasn't my abductor. He was the apprentice to Price Alexander Wells. Wells, who first tortured me in my lab and then locked me in the dungeon of his sailboat and tortured me and tortured me..."

Quinn stands, and I move backward. "Wells orchestrated everything so Simon would take the fall. But that's not all..." I turn my head, swear, and force my eyes to meet his. "Wells didn't die from ingesting shellfish toxin. He was murdered. I

100

buried the evidence. I doctored the COD report. To protect—"

"Sadie." Quinn's voice is a dark boom rattling through me.

My mouth hangs open. I wasn't going to reveal her part. I was going to take the full blame. Accept all consequences. I still can. "It was me."

"No, it wasn't." Quinn approaches me slowly, a hunter scenting his prey. His eyes take in every nervous muscle tick. "You said you were tired of lying? Stop now."

Shit. I dig my hands into my hair, claw at my scalp, unable to look into those knowing eyes. Quinn grabs my chin and angles my face toward his. The rough pads of his fingers abrasive against my skin.

"Price Wells," he says through gritted teeth. "One of the lawyers from Lark and Gannet."

I nod against his grip. "Yes."

His other hand latches on to my arm, restraining me in place. "And you're a part of this conspiracy."

Pain lances my chest, sucking the air from my lungs. But I manage, "Yes."

He releases me all at once, and I stumble back. Catching my balance, I prop my hands on the dresser. "Quinn…"

He turns his back to me. "Get out."

The ache in my chest is unbearable. Suffocating, hacking away at my soul. I shake all over, every muscle and nerve a mess of spasms. I'm afraid to move. If I do, I'll fall apart. "Don't you want an explanation?"

He rebounds so quickly, turning to face me and stalking

forward, I cringe against the dresser. "There's nothing about this you can explain or *justify*…" He spits the word at me, the fire in his eyes liquefying me beneath his furious blaze.

Tentatively, because I have nothing left to lose, I pry my fingers from the edge of the dresser and reach up. My hand trembles as I lay it against his chest.

His ragged breathing intensifies. "Avery…I'm warning you."

I can't stop. I want to know. If this is the last time Quinn will ever be this close to me, I *have* to know. A quake rolls through me. With unsteady fingers, I carefully unbutton one, then two buttons of his shirt. By the time I reach the third, my heart threatens to tear through the cartilage of my chest.

He allows me to push aside his shirt and reveal the tattooed script imprinted on his flesh. My fingers trace the slightly beveled letters, the warmth beneath my hand searing.

At his best, man is the noblest of all animals; separated from law and justice he is the worst.

"Aristotle," I whisper. My gaze flicks up to capture his penetrating stare regarding me. "There is a higher court than courts of justice, and that's the court of conscience. It supersedes all other courts."

Quinn's features contort painfully. "You think Gandhi would approve of your actions? Is your conscience completely clear of what you and Sadie have done?"

I flatten my hand over the verse. Thunderous and wild, his heartbeat rockets against my palm. "No, not at all." I stare into his heated gaze. "If I felt what I did wasn't wrong, if I could live with it...I wouldn't be chancing everything right now by telling you."

My legs go weak. No longer able to hold myself up, exhaustion and depletion of adrenaline claim my limbs. I'm falling.

A deep groan barrels free as he anchors his hands to my waist. Then I'm lifted up and seated on the dresser, my face forced level with his. My breath catches.

"What am I supposed to do?" His eyes search me, but I'm not entirely sure he's asking—more demanding I give him some answer that makes sense of this for him.

"I don't know," I admit. "All I know is...I love you and it's killing me." I squeeze my eyes closed, the hot stream of tears scorching my cheeks. "I'm so wrong for you, but I can't stop wanting you. You're the only certain thing in my life."

My parents died when I was in college. I never had anyone close to me after that—never wanted anyone close. The only certainty I could depend on was me. Until Quinn.

I can't look. Keeping my eyes sealed, I refuse to see the disappointment and hurt I know he wears. The pain I've put there. He expels a heavy breath, filling the wary air between us with heartache, and that one action sounds so defeated—defeated and lost—my misery is complete.

"I'm taking you to bed."

I open my eyes then, just in time to glimpse the smoldering of his irises. It steals what's left of my strength, and when his

103

hands capture my face, I fall into him. Off balance, giving myself over fully.

Quinn inhales deeply, resting his forehead to mine. I can feel the war raging within him—the fight between giving in to his heroic side, where he does enclose those arms around me and shelters me from my own sins, and doing what he believes is ultimately right.

Like the tattoo marking his chest; Quinn lives by a code. And that code leaves no room for a broken woman whose lax morals created the mess we're facing.

"Look at me," Quinn orders as he pulls away.

For a second, I savor the press of his hot breath against my lips before I cast my gaze upward.

"We're not figuring this out tonight." He brushes aside the trail of tears dampening my cheek. "You need rest." He releases my face and his arms surround me, cradling me against his chest in one strong move.

I bury my face against him, desperate—unwilling to think of being removed. All too soon, though, I'm lying in his bed, where he pulls back the covers and tucks me beneath the cool sheets.

I clasp his hand as he's turning away. "Stay."

He doesn't turn around, only squeezes my hand in answer, before he moves out of my touch. My heart constricts, my desperation flaring. "You said…"

He stalls at the lamp, waiting.

"You said even my scars were beautiful. But my scars aren't

just skin-deep, Quinn." Maybe the scars marring my soul are too hideous, too tainted for him to see past.

He flips off the light. I watch him exit the room, leaving me to despise the silence.

CHAPTER 11

ID

ALPHA

*T*hink about the thing you want most—the one thing that will fulfill you. Not the dream car, spouse, home, kids… Fuck the mundane. What is your greedy little black heart's desire?

Now break it down. What would it take to obtain it? Chances are, there's one common denominator for everyone: money. If you dream big enough, we're talking a certain kind of money. A special brand of green.

Wealth.

There are seven billion people on the planet. A record high. And only a pocket of humans in existence can truly call themselves wealthy.

Why is this wealth not more evenly distributed across the globe?

Because when faced with the challenges put before them,

most fail to overcome their obstacles. You have to tear down barriers, eradicate the competition, stop at nothing to obtain your goal.

Very few possess this quality.

Do you want to know the secret?

It is the id. The id is greedy by nature. The id wants what it wants and has no moral limitations. The id is the most basic, carnal aspect of our personality. It demands to be satisfied. Leave it to Freud to name this selfish beast, giving credence to our pleasure principle.

We all harbor this demon—but it's only the select few who will feed it, nurture it, and benefit from it.

I think about the id often, whenever confronted with new challenges. Like a certain gluttonous leach who's been feeding off my territory. Suckling at my empire. Slowly draining my revenue.

My ego would have me ignore him; he's a little pissant, nothing more than an irritant. He's not worthy of my attention. But my id knows better. It scents a possible threat to the ecosystem that's feeding it. And it demands to be satisfied.

"Our seven novices are right on time." I tap the screen and enlarge the image. The cameras at the marina aren't of the best quality, but I'm able to make out the gluttonous leach boarding the vessel. Slicked back hair. Tailored suit. Too much jewelry. Classic ghetto chic. I scoff. He watches too many movies. "And so is our friend."

Donovan loads a round into his gun. "Should I shake him

up a bit?"

It wouldn't be a bad idea; make the pick-up more interesting. Let him believe he's truly making his mark on my territory. "Have the boys send him a greeting," I say, panning the camera to the boat. "But make sure he sets up at the warehouse on time. I want to stay on schedule."

Donavan collects more ammunition, then sets off.

When the first girl is carted off the boat, I feel a stab of regret. I'm always there to greet my girls. I inspect all merchandise and oversee the branding personally. Exceptions must be made, however. My current circumstance prevents my participation.

I zoom in, getting a glimpse of my signature on the girl's thigh. My hands tighten on the device. I don't like doing things out of order. Having my routine disrupted. But I'm willing to accept this detour from my original objective to achieve my overall goal.

A panicked shout sounds from the back. Of course, there's still plenty of hands-on work to be done here.

I trace my finger over the screen, along each young face, giving my beauties a farewell before I kill the link to the camera feed. I set the tablet down, take a swig of bourbon, then make my way toward the back room.

The desperate pleas and screams become louder the closer I get. I've just unlocked the door and entered, and already one is clinging to my leg.

"Por favor!" she wails. "Por favor déjame ir!" Her fingers

claw at my pants.

"Her nails need to be trimmed," I tell Micah as I lean down and grip a handful of her hair. I drag her aside. No kicking her away—I don't want to bruise my girls before they're displayed.

She curls into a ball in the corner, covering her nearly naked body with her arms. I'm not heartless. I grab one of the blankets and then settle near her. "Déjame ver."

She shakes her head, ratty hair concealing her face. I'm pressed for time. I don't have the patience to soothe her feelings. "I said, let me see." I yank her leg out from underneath her and turn her so I can see the brand along her hip.

"Very nice." I toss the blanket at her, then turn toward Micah. He's running a handheld torch over the branding iron. Only the best for my girls; none of that electric heat nonsense.

The tip of the iron glows like a beautiful molten ember.

I step over the bound girl on the floor, hover near her head. "Relax," I say, smoothing her hair back. She's quivering like a tautly strung bowstring, her muffled sobs just audible through the tape covering her mouth.

Micah prepares to place the iron, and I lift her head so she can see it coming. Fear seizes her body. She struggles against the restraints. "Hold still. Don't want to mess up your brand. We'll have to do it again on the other leg."

I lean in close to her ear. "And you don't want to know the method for removing a botched branding." I lick her earlobe.

Tears leak from her eyes. And despite the searing pain attacking her body, she composes herself rather well. Oh, she's going to make me a lot of money.

My id is pleased.

I stand and move slowly through the room, checking shackles on wrists. Inspecting brandings. Yes, I'm pleased.

"They need a good scrubbing." I sniff at the air. They stink of urine. Filthy whores. "But we're nearly ready to go to auction."

I unshackle the petite brunette I've come to favor. She's learned not to fight or beg. She's smarter than the rest; I see it in the way she watches the other girls. Observes me. Examining what will earn a punishment, what gets rewarded.

She trails my lead to the bathroom where I begin filling the tub. I pat the edge of the porcelain, and she timidly sits, tucking her hands between her thighs.

She plays the part of innocence well. I let an easy smile grace my lips.

"We become different people around others," I say, letting my hand slip into the water to test the temperature. "We listen, we adapt, we project. Sometimes, we have to shave off the sharp edges when we need others to receive us as softer."

I nod to her dirty tank top and panties. She obediently discards them.

"We're also blessed with the ability to thicken those edges, sharpen them into a fine point. It's more than our survival instincts—it's the id. You remember I explained this to you?"

She nods demurely, so precious, so soft.

"Of course you do. You listen."

Her big brown eyes absorb my actions. She's rapt by my words, gauging me, deciphering what I want so she can give it to me. This will work well for her later, when her owner demands something of her. In time, she'll be able to predict his needs. Anticipate his desires.

And then, it will work not so well for me when he removes his business once she's learned how to manipulate him. She may even attempt to kill him one night after she's convinced him to trust her. Let her roam freely. Bring her to bed with him.

"It's not a difficult thing to do; discovering what people want. What will give you access to their trust." I help guide her into the water. "Even the most guarded person harbors the need to be known. It's a basic human necessity—part of the id. We're not born into this world alone; we're designed at birth to crave interaction, and we depend on others to fulfill certain needs."

I pump a dollop of shampoo onto my palm and then soothingly work it into her ratty hair. At first, she's tense. Her eyes fight to stay open. She knows better than to give herself over to comforts, to let her guard down. But as I massage her scalp, tenderly lathering the shampoo into her hair, she relaxes. Her eyes drift shut.

"You're extra perceptive to this," I tell her. "You'll use your instincts and wits to survive. Even prosper in your circumstance. You'll become a favorite."

"Then—" I rest my sudsy hands on her shoulders "—you'll

111

be tempted to want more."

I push her below the water. Hold her under. Her arms and legs thrash at the water. Her body bucks and battles against my grip.

I bring her up. "I can't have even one smart cunt tarnish my name and business." I submerge her again.

I don't just offer my clients a product; I offer them a superior product.

Broken and ready to be rebuilt to their own making.

When her fight begins to weaken, her grasp on my wrists going slack, I use my thumbs to pry her eyes open. She stares at me through the water, through her fear. She'll never forget this feeling.

And, when I finally drag her above the water, gasping for air, tears blending with the water soaking her skin, I snatch her hair and haul her close. "Never forget who made you. You won't ever belong to any of those men." I kiss her lips affectionately. Stroke the fresh brand along her thigh.

"You're mine. Always."

CHAPTER 12

GRAVE

QUINN

A s a detective, I depend on particular skillsets to uncover the truth. I've honed my instincts to be extra perceptive. I pride myself in knowing when a perp is lying. I enjoy making them sweat, turning up the heat, watching them unravel.

Since the close of the serial killer case, I've been aware that not every convenient detail surrounding Simon Whitmore was as clear-cut as it was documented. Against my nature, I made a conscious choice to ignore the annoying points that didn't quite line up. I postponed delving into the past in order to protect someone I care about.

It was the hardest choice of my career.

Sleepless nights plagued me as my brain churned the facts, trying to link Simon to Lyle Connelly. Yet deep down, I knew Sadie was the link—even if I had no evidence. She was hiding the variable that would tie their connection together.

That variable's name was Price Wells.

He was the missing link.

That night in the hospital, when I sat beside Sadie, as we both waited to hear on Avery's condition, I could've asked—and in that moment, Sadie would have told me the truth. But if she had, I would've been bound by my Oath of Honor to bring her actions to light.

I've been able to move forward by telling myself I didn't pursue it because Sadie needed to be protected. I wanted—and *still* want—to believe she killed Connelly in self-defense.

We all lie to ourselves. That's the real maddening truth.

And I'm the biggest liar of all. I believed I was carrying this burden for her. But selfishly, I didn't want the full burden placed on me, to be the one to exhume the past and have the crippling truth stare me right in the face:

My partner is a killer.

I'm just as guilty as Sadie and Avery by my own omission.

I can't recall who first told me that omission is just a convenient form of betrayal—but it's as true now as ever, and it's time to stop lying.

I've been parked out front of the precinct for half an hour, contemplating, deciding my next action. I left my apartment this morning before Avery awoke. Left her a box of green tea and honey that I picked up for her on the counter. With a note:

Don't leave until your detail arrives to escort you to work.

Bitter, chaste. Strictly business. The words of a colleague

and not a lover. Not even a friend. Part of me—the part that stopped Sadie from revealing the truth—wanted to crawl into bed with Avery last night and make love to her until her pain fled. Chase away her darkness. Reassure her that I'll always protect her.

But the part of me that took an oath all those years ago couldn't give in so easily. I'm a bastard, I know. Who turns their back on the woman they love after she just confessed her sins? Hell, after she confessed she loved me.

I'm a fucking bastard.

I touch the folded letter tucked in my coat pocket. I think about pulling it out, reading it again. Instead, I drop my hand, leaving Avery's words to fester right next to my heart.

She must have been half delirious with exhaustion when she wrote it. What does she want me to do? Turn it in? Let her take the whole wrap for Wells?

If I was half the man she needs…I'd tear the letter up. Burn it. Stomp on the ashes.

Hell, it's not a true confession, anyway. It's fabricated. Meant to protect Sadie. I don't need my keen detective skills to decipher the lies, but they help.

They help so well I can suss out just what role Sadie did play. Without Sadie, Avery never would've known who her true abductor was—she wouldn't be suffering the torment she's suffering now. Her conscience tearing her apart. Had Sadie not taken the law into her own hands, and had come to me with the truth, Wells would be in prison. Avery would be safe. And

115

the only one in danger of their past would be Sadie.

Shit. I've fucking come full circle.

A knock on my window drags me out of my self-loathing, and I turn to see Carson standing beside my car. His glum expression sums up how all of this has gone to shit. I motion for him to back away as I open the door and step out, well aware of what he's about to ask. He's been blowing up my phone all morning.

"I'm not turning you in. Yet," I tell him, and the tension in his shoulders immediately diminishes.

"Thank you, Detective Quinn. But...why not?" He's dressed like he's applying for his first job. White dress shirt starched. Slacks ironed. He came in prepared to fight for his job. Ready to impress me.

Good. He should be on point, but in all honesty, after I left Avery in my bed last night, the thought of Carson being the department leak hasn't crossed my mind once. And if I report him now, I'll have to make a firm decision on my own culpable actions.

That's not why I'm here.

"Contrary to popular belief," I say, "I do give more than one chance, Carson. You're a good detective with some bad habits." I stare down at him. "That's a recipe for a dirty cop."

"I know," he says, lowering his gaze. "I have been getting help. You know, for the gambling."

He can't look me in the eye. He's lying, but right now, there's bigger issues than his personal problems to conquer.

"Just don't make me regret it."

When his eyes meet mine, I at least know he means to try. "I won't, boss." He rubs the back of his neck, glancing around. "Any word on tonight?"

I direct my gaze on the precinct. "I'll know in about ten minutes."

Carson wasn't exaggerating when he said the department was crawling with black suits. The FBI Organized Crime Division has their own damn headquarters not ten miles away, and yet they've taken over my department.

The turf invaders are using our resources. But why?

I halt Carson with the back of my hand to his chest. "The bond hearing yesterday – what happened during the questioning?"

Carson's features pull together. "There was no questioning. Shit. Avery said not to tell you—"

I cross my arms, eyes narrowed hard on him.

He scratches the back of his head, as if he's digging the answers out. "The perps are out on bond. Maddox got them out on some bullshit claim of accidental imprisonment. Stating according to them, Avery was already inside the van when they 'borrowed' it."

Anger spikes my blood. The pieces all trickle down from there. During the hearing, Avery will have to testify to the fact she was kidnapped from the lab. Maddox and his slimy clients are counting on her not doing so, because the Alpha is threatening to expose her for altering evidence on Wells' death. Maybe even try to frame her for his murder.

"You know it won't stick," Carson says, interrupting my thoughts. "There's no way a judge will buy that shit."

Not in a just world, where criminals don't have judges in their pockets—but we can't trust a system that's already proven to be corrupt.

"Is there surveillance on the perps now?" I ask.

"At least two unis," he says, eyebrows drawn together in question.

"Okay. Good. Collect all intel from them and then stay put in your office until I call you."

"I can do that." He turns toward me. "What are you going to do?"

What I have to.

"I'll contact you soon," I say as I take off toward Wexler's office.

Not even a full two days, and I'm crawling back to the only thing I know. I don't give a shit what it looks like—if every person on this floor pities the pathetic has-been detective. I'm not moving forward without my badge.

I knock on the captain's door. When it opens, I'm not surprised to see a couple of Feds inside, despite hoping to do this in private. "Captain?"

He looks washed-out. His gray hair mussed, and he's

wearing the same clothes from yesterday. He motions me through the doorway. "Just in time," he says. "Come on in."

As I enter, the two Feds nod to me in greeting. I'm well acquainted with Agent Rollins, but the woman with long dark hair to his left I can't place.

"Special Agent Rollins you've met. He was a great help to us on the previous serial killer case. And this is Special Agent Bell."

She extends her hand. "Lena," she says, and I raise my brows. "Yes, I know. Lena Bell. My name is a little sing-song." She smiles warmly as I shake her hand. "My mother was a bit different."

Vague and open at the same time. A difficult combination to pull off, but this agent does it with style. "You're the head of the Organized Crime Division."

Her smile spreads easily, making her the brightest thing in Wexler's drab office. "I am, detective. Good instincts. That's precisely why I've requested to bring you back in."

Requested. I look at Wexler for confirmation on this. From his overworked appearance, I'd say she hardly requested nicely. The captain settles behind his desk and opens a drawer. "You've been officially reinstated, Quinn." He places my gun and badge on the desk.

Like Carson, I came here with one purpose: to fight for my job. To make sure that what transpires next is upheld within the parameters of the law. I'd be lying if I didn't admit I'm somewhat disappointed. I had a whole speech prepared and everything, and I'm still locked and loaded.

Relaxing my stiff shoulders, I bury my rebuttal with a heavy exhale. "I appreciate your confidence in me." It comes out more condescending than I intend.

"I never lost confidence in you," Wexler states. "You do understand that reprimands have to be issued. This was far less severe than it could've been—"

"But there are more pressing circumstances than dangerous highway pursuits," Agent Bell interrupts. "In the Bureau, your methods used to rescue Doctor Johnson would've been received with praise rather than reprimand. As such, I'm convinced that we need you on this investigation, Detective Quinn."

I holster my gun in my shoulder harness and tuck my badge into the inseam of my coat. I take a moment to appreciate the feel of being reinstated, complete as a detective, before turning toward the agent. "Then you're aware of how I operate," I say, measuring her facial response. "My partner and I work alone."

She must be as skilled as I am at schooling her features. As hard as that statement was to make about Sadie—as difficult as it is to openly stand by her, having confirmed my worst suspicions—I did so with the cool confidence of a detective with nothing to hide, and the agent doesn't bat an eye or tick a muscle.

"Although the Bureau is inclined to see things done with a certain order," she says, closing the gap between us. "I realize that each of my agents have their own skills, their own methods, in which they operate."

I stare into her eyes, aware of the awkwardness our standoff is creating for the other two men in this office. "I'm not one of your agents."

Here, her lips do twitch. A slight smile pulls into place. "Doesn't mean we can't work well together, detective."

I should ask what she needs from this department. She obviously requires the cooperation from my team, which is the only reason why I've been reinstated. She needs me to corral the officers, get them in line and onboard. Operating under her command.

I should ask—but it might be more interesting to watch it play out.

I match her smile. "I think we will work quite well together, Agent Bell. I'm at your disposal."

Her tongue traces her bottom lip before her smile widens. I let my gaze be drawn to her full lips and that action, giving her what she wants; a sense of control over me. "Great," she says. "Let's get to work."

I glance over at Wexler, who's unable to mask his anxiousness. He should be concerned. He's just let a whole lot of trouble walk right into his precinct. Agent Bell heads into the bullpen, and I follow closely behind.

Allowing Special Agent Lena Bell to address the task force

was easier and less painful than I thought it would be. She took the reins, grouping unis and detectives into individual teams with their own assignments.

Even during the serial killer case, I refused to let Agent Proctor call all the shots. The last side op I orchestrated with Sadie could've gotten her killed, and I was attacked. I'm not above admitting when I make a mistake, and I'd like to believe I learn from them. So this time, I'm more than capable of hanging back and letting the big dogs set the pace.

You learn more when you watch.

Maybe it's me getting older, having run low on that young blood testosterone that demands I chase after every suspect, but if I've discovered anything from the previous case, it's this: narcissists will make themselves known.

I don't have to chase down every one, throwing my weight around. Tackling every suspect and beating answers out. If you listen closely, they'll reveal the answers. They can't help but want to be heard.

Once Agent Bell wraps up the task force meeting, sending the teams on their way, she approaches me with a phone. "This is your direct line to me." She takes my hand in hers and places the phone in my palm. She doesn't release me right away, her hand too soft and small compared to my rough, large one.

"I know this is difficult for you," she continues. "Everyone here cares for Doctor Johnson and wants to see her safe, but you especially."

I pull my hand free and slide the phone into my breast

pocket. "I don't think it takes special intelligence to uncover that fact and state the obvious."

A tight smile seams her lips together. "Human trafficking cases are never easy, Quinn. Couple that with a serial killer amid this case, and that makes it even harder. I've worked many trafficking cases, and every time, there's a painful tradeoff. You lose a part of yourself with each one." She sighs. "It's either that, or never be able to sleep. You have to harden yourself in ways that separate you from the people you care about."

I tilt my head, really studying her. "Are you trying to warn me about something?"

She touches my arm. "It can get lonely. And I realize you're an island. You've said yourself that you work best alone." She caresses my arm tenderly. "You're a leader, and leaders suffer isolation like no other. I don't want this case to do that to you. I want you to know that I understand…that I can relate to that loneliness."

Mother of mercy. Talk about head shrinking. I'd be scared to put her and Sadie in the same room together. I offer her a genuine smile to diffuse some of my discomfort. "I appreciate your concern, Agent—"

"Lena," she states.

"Ah, Lena." I scrub the back of my neck, heat splashing my face. "But I did say that I work with a partner. Thank you, though. If I have any questions or concerns, I know where to bring them."

"Anytime," she says. "My proverbial door is always open

to you."

Jesus. I watch her saunter off toward Wexler, her hips swinging, long legs eating up the floor with each sultry step. If she lays it on me that heavily, I worry about the poor bastard she really puts in her sights.

I'm not the only one who picked up on what she was dropping. Sadie stands at the door to my office, her arms crossed, one eyebrow cocked.

Hell. Of course she saw.

I head her way and open my door, standing to the side as I nod her inside. "Don't start—"

"If that scene got any hotter, I'd have to douse you with a bucket of ice water." She tilts her head. "And someone should hose her down for sure."

For the moment, I let her have her victory. "I think that's her way of keeping tabs."

She smirks. "I thought you were more perceptive than that."

I shake my head. "Why are you here?"

Her head jerks back. "Why am I here? The FBI are heading up a full investigation into a criminal network they believe are in charge of the major human trafficking in Virginia. Right here, in this department." She eases closer to me. "And we have intel on an auction that happens to be taking place tonight."

I lean back against my desk, cross my arms. "So we let the Feds handle it."

The shock on her face would cause me physical pain any

other day. Sadie's disappointed glower can bring a man to his knees. But not today.

"You're really going to hand over control to the Feds. Put Avery's fate in their hands."

"Is that what I'm doing?" I straighten to my full height and look down at her.

"Yes." She doesn't back down.

"And how do you think I should handle it? Set up a secret meeting with the Alpha. Slip him a poison. Watch him die. Then have Avery doctor the COD report as just another fatal accident." I brush my hands together, as if wiping them clean. "There seems to be a pattern of those accidents with your cases, Bonds."

Her eyes narrow. "I'm not surprised you discovered the truth," she says. "Just surprised it took you this long."

I mock laugh. "I didn't think your buttons could be pushed so easily. Glad to see you do reflect some human emotion."

She turns her head away, stares at the whiteboard. "Are we really doing this?"

"What?"

When she looks at me, her face is devoid of any anger. But it's also absent of hurt or emotion. She's a pro at stoicism. "I don't want us to be enemies, Quinn."

"You're right," I say, pushing off the desk. "Neither do I. I might end up dead."

"Fine." She tosses her hands in the air. "Pout. Be pissed off, righteous anger guy. But just remember, it was you who refused the truth when I offered it to you." Eyes drilled hard on me, she waits for a reaction I'm not going to give. "With or without you, I won't let Avery get hurt. She's been through hell, and I won't let her go back there."

This does trigger a reaction. "That hell? The one where she was tortured, beat with a cane for the whole department to witness? That hell she suffered was because of a fucked up situation you created when you went outside of the law to hunt and kill Lyle Connelly."

There it is. The root of my anger.

"And then," I say, "you dragged her further into that hell when you implemented her in the murder of Price Wells. You need to stop, Sadie. You need to stop before you destroy her. She's not—" I look down, jaw clenched.

"Me," she whispers in answer.

I look up and stare into her green eyes, impassive. "She's not you. That's right. She feels what you're not capable of feeling. Guilt. Remorse. Even for those who deserve the death penalty, she understands that punishment shouldn't come at her hands. It shouldn't come at any of our hands. We're not executioners."

"You're right." Sadie glances through the glass wall, shielding her face from me. Beyond this office, there's a flurry of chaos, no one aware of the battle that rages within. It's just another day on the job. Agent Bonds and Detective Quinn arguing, as usual.

But this is no ordinary struggle of wills.

I see that as soon as Sadie's able to look at me again. Eyes wide, they shimmer with something I've never seen from her before. Tears. It rips through me with brutal force, decimating and destructive.

"You're right," she says again. "I didn't want to drag her into my world, but I did. And her suffering was the consequences of my actions."

A chest-crushing exhale pushes free. "Sadie… Fuck."

"I can't change the past, Quinn. If I could, I'd have done so much differently. For Avery's sake. Back then, I never expected to feel…" She trails off, and a single tear slips free. "I never expected to feel. Period. I never thought I'd be capable of caring for others, but God. I care about Avery, and I even care about you. And I don't want to see anyone else suffer." She wipes hard at her cheek, then stares at the wetness on her hand in disbelief. "All I can do now is make sure that every loose end, that every threat, is eliminated. It's the one thing I'm good at."

She takes off toward the door. I'm there in a heartbeat to grab her arm and pull her to a stop. "I actually don't want to be your enemy, Sadie. That's not what I want for us."

She swallows hard. "But now that you know the truth, can you ever look at me the same?"

She pulls away from me, and I let her. No—I can't look at her the same. But I haven't been able to since that night

127

in the hospital. When faced with the ugly truth of a person's unvarnished existence, it takes one hell of a person to see past it.

And I'm not a saint.

"That's what I thought," she says. "If you handle the Feds, keep their attention diverted elsewhere, I'll make sure this ends tonight."

She leaves then, and all I can do is stare at the fucking floor. My mind a twisted, tangled web. Despite what I said in the heat of the moment, Sadie is exactly the hero Avery needs right now.

Someone determined to go to any extreme to protect the person they love.

Am I angry with Sadie because I really believe she's at fault, or because I envy her ability to do what's necessary at any cost?

I shut my door and pull out my phone, punch in Carson's contact. He answers on the first ring. "Head to Lark and Gannet now," I say, then end the call before he can ask questions. I make another call to Larkin before I let my mind start rationalizing.

"I'm sending Carson your way," I say to him. "Make sure he's prepped and ready to go in tonight."

"I'm impressed, detective," Larkin says, and I can hear the arrogance in his voice. He thinks he's won, that I've stepped over my hard-drawn line in the sand. "Mister Carson will be well on his way to the elite by this evening. I've already prepared additional security measures. Just think: your career will be made by the end of the night."

I hang up.

By the end of the night, I won't have a career. The plan is not to bring in the Alpha; it's to end the threat.

For good.

CHAPTER 13

IDENTITY CRISIS

AVERY

espite fighting my way into a fitful sleep, I slept undisturbed, not even stirring at three a.m. to the usual rocking—the never-ending motion of the boat that haunts my nights. Once the letter was written, and the truth as I want to present it was made manifest, my screams didn't break the night, my nightmares held back as if Quinn's hand never left mine.

Quinn had already left by the time I woke, leaving behind his own letter. Which didn't acknowledge my statement, only reiterated in his own candid, protective way that I wasn't to leave his apartment without officer detail.

I didn't need them. I planned to accept Aubrey's offer to oversee my lab so I could take the day off. I'm not needed at the lab, anyway—not really. My emotional state is causing anxiety for my techs, and I know what a hectic work environment that creates.

It's stressful enough as it is. The pressure to examine five victims and then reexamine every time new information is discovered by a detective. I usually excel under pressure, but there's a limit, and nothing within me wanted to meet that challenge this morning.

For one short moment, when I first awoke in Quinn's bed, with his masculine scent embracing me, it was bliss. A blank slate, the mind empty of all painful memories, and then the flood of awareness. The violent reminder of trying to atone for my sins was accompanied with physical pain, tangible proof that I'm mentally devolving.

I dread Sadie's reaction when she discovers I put our secret into words. Given Quinn hard evidence to tie me to Price Wells. I penned the letter to him in a fit of delirium, and I'm not even sure what I divulged—other than I took full responsibility.

Sadie's name was not mentioned. Every action she took to plot and execute Wells' demise, I claimed for myself. Regardless if Quinn will puzzle out all the altered details behind my statement, the proof I provided him will only testify that I killed my abductor.

There is liberation in acceptance.

I didn't even feel this free when I was unshackled from that dungeon.

I'm not a martyr—I don't think that highly of myself; I'm not selfless. I'm just doing what's right by the woman who avenged me.

Will I see that look in Sadie's eyes afterward? The one that pities me for being so weak?

The truth is: I'm not as strong as her. I'm not sure if that revelation calms or frightens me, but I'm at least certain in my role. I'm not her.

Wells dressed me like her, made me relive the torture she endured. She was only sixteen when she was abducted and exposed to this world's cruelty. Somehow, she survived, and she channeled her painful experience into strength, where she not only stands up to monsters like her abductor; she seeks them out. Punishes them. Her existence in this turbulent world means less people will suffer because of her.

Me? I barely escaped my dungeon. Having felt what Sadie did broke me. I put myself together for a short time, but I also used alcohol and my designer aphrodisiac just to feel normal.

Then when confronted with having to live that torture all over again…I cracked. Within twenty-four hours, I've exposed Sadie and myself, and now I'm tempted to expose us even further—

—just to make it end. Just to hear the blessed hum of silence and to make the inner voice shouting in my head shut the hell up.

"The fuming chamber is ready, Doctor Johnson," Natalie says, awakening me from my destructive daze.

I run my forearm across my brow, wiping at the clamminess of my skin. The humidity in the lab is stifling. "Thanks, Natalie. Please let Doctor Paulson know we're about to begin."

She trots off, always striving to impress. She'll make a good medical examiner in my absence. I should be alarmed at how at ease I am with that realization, but I'm not. I'm complacent.

I'm simply tired and ready for the relief that follows once I no longer have to hide my secrets. Repentance has to be the next step.

With gloved hands, I prep the hotplate, setting the temperature to 260 Fahrenheit. The process of lifting a latent fingerprint from a dead body is not an easy one. Rather, it's downright impossible, unless the body was preserved in an ideal environment. Aubrey called this morning, sure he'd discovered a possible fingerprint on the back neck area of vic number five. There was no taking today off. There was no alternative.

I have to be here.

Aside from the third vic donning my lab coat, the Alpha made no other threats—leaving me to believe the other victims were simply discarded merchandise; test subjects no longer of use. If there is an auction tonight, keeping the ACPD busy chasing a killer is an ideal distraction. A sick logic, but the Alpha sacrificed some so the rest remain unseen.

We can't even begin to speculate as to how many abducted women are still out there, either awaiting a horrific death, or about to be auctioned off.

With or without Quinn by my side tonight, I will attempt to stop this. For now, Sadie is still invested in seeing this to the end. So I can't let the masked man's threat to expose me and my role in Wells' murder prevent tonight from happening. Being taken in for questioning cannot happen. And that's why I'm here—to make sure that whatever message the Alpha may have planted on this vic remains a mystery until this is over.

I slip on my mask.

I have no doubt that the Alpha and his lackeys are practiced enough not to leave behind something so careless as a fingerprint. If there is one on this vic, I'm almost certain it was left on purpose, with the intent for me to find.

"The lab has been cleared," Aubrey says as he approaches. His glasses are in place, and he's wearing a mask. "How many times have you performed this procedure?"

I glance at Natalie, glad they're both unaware of the unsure expression I wear beneath my mask. "None," I admit. "If you haven't noticed, the M.E.'s lab isn't equipped for this kind of forensics. Usually, in a case like this, I'd have the body transported to the forensics' lab." I crack open a tube of cyanoacrylate, and drop a measured amount of superglue onto the hotplate inside the chamber.

Aubrey slowly increases the humidity level, and the chamber fills with vapor. "I'm impressed your assistants were able to build this chamber in such short notice. You have a tight and skilled crew here."

I really do. And they've managed to persevere in spite of so many setbacks and difficulties. Like when Simon was declared a serial killer. And Carmen was attacked by Simon and hospitalized. She never returned, but I don't fault her. No one does. They kept on, and that's why I know they'll brave what's to happen next.

The fumed body of the drowned vic lays face-down on the steel autopsy table. Her secrets awaiting to be revealed. The fuming process was successful; the cyanoacrylate affixed to her bloated skin without fail. And I have to wonder if her death was designed for this specific purpose; if the Alpha is so meticulous they submerged her body in water to create the perfect canvas to plant a latent fingerprint.

I watch Aubrey dust the black fingerprint powder along the back of the vic's neck, delicately twirling the wand, the bristles tapping an image to life. And there it is: one flawless print.

"That developed rather nicely," he says, pride evident in his voice.

It did develop nicely. There was some debate over whether to use magnetic powder, but in the end, we agreed the iron-rich content of the powder would be too abrasive and may wear away the print.

I should've pushed for the magnetic powder. I should've dusted the print myself. I could still save myself...if I step forward now to lift the print. Just one smudge, one slip of my fingers, and all this will go away.

I squeeze my eyes closed and quell the fiery ache gripping

135

my chest.

It's too late. Quinn already knows the truth, and he's bound by his oath to expose it. To expose *me*. That's why he didn't stay with me last night, why he couldn't face me this morning. He may be struggling with his conscience, battling when to do just that—but he will. He will do what's ultimately right.

I glance at the time on my phone and then flip on my camera. While Aubrey is preparing the reagents and lifting tape, I snap a couple shots of the print.

Soon, Aubrey has a clean, sealed fingerprint. He holds it up to the florescent light. "Don't you find it conspicuous that a lone print was found in this particular place." He tilts the screen, angling his head. "It doesn't make sense. You don't move a body by the neck. Why would a print be there?"

I suck in a sharp breath. "I see this place has you speculating and working out theories," I say, masking the quiver in my voice.

He looks at me, a thin smile on his handsome face. "Touché." He lowers the screen and places it in a manila folder. "Should get this to the actual case solvers right away. Would be even more surreal to actually get a hit from this print on one of the databases."

And my stomach bottoms out. That's exactly what I fear: the unknown—the element of surprise.

"Keep me posted." I turn to head toward my office.

"Don't you want to come with?" he asks.

I pause. "I have a couple reports to finish in my office, and then…I don't know." I shrug. "I may just actually take the rest of the day off."

His smile warms. "I think that's a good idea, Avery. I'll message you with any updates."

I return his smile before I take off, my breath held until I'm able to lock my office door behind me. I release the air from my lungs in a hard expel, lightheaded. The FBI M.E. has turned out to be an asset rather than a hindrance, and it pains me that I can't enjoy this shared learning experience between us.

Pulling my laptop from my bag, I set up on my desk quickly. I have the image of the print scanned into my program and running a search before I can talk myself out of it.

I keep copies of the lab files in a program I coded myself for easy reference. And when I get a hit, my chest implodes. Light and sound flickers in and out.

A face rolls across the screen, a red flashing print to its right.

Price Alexander Wells.

"Fuck."

I'm sure there are many other, more elegant ways to express my world falling down around me, but not this second.

I'm fucked.

Not even Quinn will be able to explain away how a dead man's fingerprint ended up on a murder victim.

CHAPTER 14

THE SUMMIT

QUINN

hen I look back over my life, after I've become an old retired, washed-out detective with a back brace and arthritic joints, I wonder if this moment—this pivotal moment—will be my ultimate failure or biggest triumph.

A triumph over myself, that is, for making my own rules, not being afraid to go against the grain of justice to protect those I love.

Either way, I won't regret my choice. Some things we just have to accept in spite of ourselves. Who we originally believed we wanted to be.

I imagine Sadie had to have given herself this lecture at some point. Right before she made a decisive judgment call to kill a perpetrator who would otherwise go unpunished, would continue to hurt and murder, and she rationalized if she didn't do it, didn't tip the scales of justice in her favor, the injustice would continue.

Hell, I don't know if she ever battled her conscience at all. Maybe it was as easy as flipping a coin for her; heads she knifes them, tails she shoots them.

I scrub my hands down my face, detesting the smell of leather and coffee filtering through Larkin's building. The main conference room has become a surveillance hub, equipped with numerous monitors and equipment I'm not even sure how Larkin got his hands on.

I don't want to know. I'm here for one purpose, and when that purpose walks into the room, my heart fucking stops.

I recognize Avery—but if you didn't know her, really know her, then she'd float through the room as a tantalizing stranger. Her blond hair is now a thick, rich auburn brown. Her face glows, a fair porcelain, with contrasting dark makeup shadowing her eyes and lips. Smoky and elegant, she's any man's fantasy.

She wraps her arms around her waist, shrinking beneath a satin dress, but Alexis pushes Avery's hands back to her sides, forcing her to lift her head and look the part of a bought and owned sex toy.

My feet are moving me toward her before my brain catches up.

"Only bow your head when you're in the presence of your Master," Alexis tells Avery. "Don't talk to any other men unless Carson gives you permission. Don't look into their eyes; that's

139

an insult to your Master."

Alexis continues to give Avery instructions as my eyes rake over the black dress and exposed skin. The scars I felt along that skin have been concealed, along with the deep gash that runs the length of her bottom lip and chin. My fingers curl into fists as I tamp down the urge to run my thumb over her lips and wipe the makeup away.

I want to see all of her.

Avery's eyes flick up and latch on to my gaze. "With the mask, I think this will work," she says. "No one there should recognize me."

Alexis glances between us and, noticing the tension, assesses Avery quickly before she decides it's all right to leave her side. "I'll go check on how Carson's doing. We'll go over a couple more things before it's time."

"Thank you," I say to her as she starts to walk off, and she returns my leaden gratitude with a tight smile. As Avery is determined to do this, at least it seems she's getting instructions that will keep her safe.

And I'll be right here, on the other side of the monitor, just minutes away should anything go wrong.

Still… "You don't have to do this," I say. "There's still time to inform the Feds."

She shakes her head, her soft, newly dyed tresses whispering over her creamy shoulders. My throat constricts. "We can't chance that something will go wrong, that the Alpha would be alerted. If the auction doesn't happen as planned, we might not get the chance to find him again."

She's right. I could retrieve the phone Special Agent Bell gave me right now; it's a trigger ready to be pulled. But at what cost? Those women's lives? Avery's? When we apprehend the Alpha and his accomplices, it will not be in The Firm.

I can't risk the Feds rushing in and blowing this op.

"I know this is the last place you want to be." She reaches out, but drops her hand just as fast. "But thank you. I feel better…safer knowing you'll be watching. Even if…"

I take her hand in mine, trace my thumb over her wrist. "Even if tomorrow I have to start an investigation into Wells?"

She flinches, but doesn't pull away. I'm an asshole for saying his name so nonchalantly, like it doesn't effect her. Like he's not the sick fuck who tortured her…nearly *killed* her. A real man would be livid that he didn't kill the fucker himself.

Am I less than a real man? Because I haven't thanked Sadie for wiping his fucking sadistic existence off the face of the planet? If so, I guess it's one more thing I'll have to come to terms with in my later years.

"Exactly," she finally says. "And I'm not worried, Quinn. I know you'll have to do the right thing, and I'm ready to face that."

Her letter rests heavily in my inseam pocket, pressed like a weight against my chest. "Let's get through tonight first," is all I can say.

She's quick to nod. "Okay. But there's something else you need to know."

My stomach rocks at her words. I'm not sure I can handle any more confessions.

"We discovered a print on the fifth victim today," she says, jumping straight in. "The print was sent to the techs to run a search, but I knew…I just knew." She releases a strained breath and steals her hand away from mine. "It's Price Wells' fingerprint. I'm not sure how the Alpha got it, but it was planted on the body."

I'm correlating too many theories at once, none of them obvious as to why the Alpha would bring Wells into the picture. Except one: "The Alpha knows."

Her eyes glisten with the reflection of low monitor light. "The masked man who took me. Yes. He knew. I now believe he was the same person who contacted me on the forum… but I didn't do what he demanded. I changed the COD reports on the vics, stating they weren't accidents. I was told if I didn't cooperate, that they'd make it known what I did…" She trails off.

And that's ultimately why she's putting herself at risk. She feels responsible for those women—that her actions somehow resulted in their fate. I'm no damn psychologist, but I'm sure it's some form of misplaced guilt; her darknet activity was not the catalyst. And her doctoring Wells' COD report is not to blame.

The people behind the crimes are.

Piecing together how this criminal network has any connection to Wells will take time. More time than I have this instant. There's too many questions that need answers. But I only have one for Avery. "Is this why you're doing this tonight?" I hold her gaze. "To silence the Alpha."

Her features twist into an incensed expression. "No. Of course not. If that were the case, I'd have left the COD reports alone. I'd have never told you the truth."

The vise compressing my chest loosens a fraction. "All right."

She blinks, a stunned expression wiping away her anger.

For what it's worth, I believe her. Until Avery was abducted and her whole world consumed with fear and pain, she was the most professional, moral person I knew. She still is... Only I'm not sure how much of Sadie's influence is responsible for her actions.

Fuck it all to hell. I've come this far—I'll see this through. I have no other choice.

"Don't think about the fingerprint or Wells or anything else while you're in there." I clasp her face, stare into her dark gaze. "Just focus on keeping yourself safe."

She swallows, and I feel the force of it pulse against my fingers. Her lips part, her breath hot against my skin, but before she's able to voice her thoughts, we're interrupted.

With effort, I pull back as Carson and Larkin enter the conference room. Carson is decked out in an expensive suit, with a label I doubt I'd recognize. Larkin looks smug, proud of his transformation of the rookie into an entrepreneur of human slave acquiring.

"Real nice," I say as Carson adjusts his tie. "You'll fit right in—" I eye Larkin "—with the rest of the deviant pervs."

The lawyer's not thrown by my comment. He actually smiles, brushing off my sarcasm like he brushes off his designer suit. "Your detective cleans up well. And I'll take that as a compliment."

Alexis reenters and begins briefing both Carson and Avery on more of the nuances and etiquette of the club, and I find Sadie and Colton checking the surveillance equipment. Seems to me they should be in on the prep work.

When Carson steps away from the group, I'm there to intercept him. I brace a hand on the back of his neck and pull him in close. "It should go without saying, but I'm going to make it real fucking clear." I grip his neck. "Avery doesn't get hurt. Not a scratch. Not a bruise. Not one finger—from *anyone*—touches her. Are we clear?"

He gives his head a nod against my hold. "Crystal, boss."

I smack the back of his head. "I know you'll keep her safe," I say, leaving the rest unsaid of what will happen if he doesn't. I think we're on the same page.

I've about got myself composed when a blond man enters the room, and my hackles rise. "This op was supposed to be strictly confidential. Who's that?"

Colton steps forward. "My roommate."

"And my personal driver," Larkin follows up. "Who I trust to keep this secret. We need another ally to make this work, and I can vouch for Jefferson."

Vouch. One snake vouching for another. Mother fuckers. Of course they'd all be connected. The underground world of BDSM and fetishes…swapping out partners and roommates and drivers. I glance at Sadie with raised eyebrows. This stinks of something foul, and I don't like it.

"I wasn't actually aware that Jefferson worked for Larkin until just recently," Sadie says, as if she's reading my mind. "Neither was Colton. It's as much a surprise to us, but we do need another person, Quinn. Just in case."

Just in case Larkin decides to pull something while in The Firm, to make sure he has a man of his own here to carry out instructions. Check. Keep the status quo.

Soon as this is done, and I have one moment of peace, I'm launching a full-scale investigation into every last one of them. I'm going to map out this law firm and uncover every dirty secret and deed.

As they get Jefferson set up before a monitor, I feel the press of a hand in mine. The sudden caress startles me, and I look over at Avery. "Maybe one day, when this is over…" she says. She places a tender kiss to my knuckles. They're still scratched and bruised from pounding my fist into one of the perps. "Then you'll look at me the way you did before."

She's gone before I can reply, taking the air in my lungs with her. But her message is clear: maybe one day this will be behind us and we'll have another chance. I swallow down the burning ache, pushing it into the pit of my gut.

Putting my head in the game, I watch everything closely.

145

Sadie places a tiny earbud in Avery's ear. Alexis fastens a collar around Avery's neck that houses a camera. Colton and Larkin take these same measures with Carson, making sure his virtually invisible surveillance pieces are in place and operational.

This is our eyes and ears into The Firm.

This is my only connection to Avery.

Once they're ready, I move to the hallway and watch Avery meet Carson, Larkin, and Alexis at the elevator. Avery steps inside the elevator car and turns, her eyes seeking mine. She doesn't look away. She stays with me until the silver doors close, then she's gone.

CHAPTER 15

THE FIRM

AVERY

*T*he limo pulls to a stop before the Skylark Hotel. It's beautiful and graceful with a slim, soaring tower, and not at all what I expected.

I duck my head to stare out of the tinted window, my gaze following the many reflective floors shimmering with city lights to the top.

"I felt the same way when I first saw it," Alexis says.

I glance at her. "Surprised?"

She smiles. "Completely. Not what you expected, is it?"

I shake my head to confirm that this is nothing like what I pictured while I was being prepped to enter as a member into a secret sex society. A hiss of static erupts in my ear, then Quinn's voice announces he's testing the connection.

Larkin places a finger to his ear. "We hear you, detective. Now, please don't monopolize the feed. It will be difficult enough without a cop in all our ears."

"It's not too late to call this off and take a different route," Quinn says. I can hear the urgency in his voice, and I admit, staring at the hotel, uncertain about what's within...what comes next...I almost agree to do just that.

"Do you want to catch the minnow or the big fish?" Larkin asks, directing his question to the man on the other end of the feed. "You yourself said if the FBI enters the picture, they'll storm in all halfcocked."

A moment of tense silence. Then: "You better be sure, Larkin." A beat. "I want nothing less than to collar the head of this criminal network. Tonight," Quinn adds.

Larkin looks around the cab of the limo, capturing each of our gazes. "Collar? As much as I enjoy cop jargon, let's be clear." He snaps his fingers, and the driver opens Larkin's door. He steps out and straightens his tie. "Collaring means something entirely different in this world, detective."

With that, Larkin extends his hand and helps Alexis from the limo. Carson settles his hand over mine on my knee, and I look up. "It's all right to be nervous," he says.

"Are you?"

His hollow laugh fills the car. "I'm taking *you* into The Firm, with Quinn watching my every move. Nervous is a strong understatement."

My face flushes. Carson's a detective, so of course he's *detected* the tension between Quinn and I. We're more than obvious to anyone who looks close enough.

"Hey," he says, gripping my hand reassuringly. "Remember, if it becomes too much, if there're any triggers, just say the word."

"Lemon," I say, and he smiles. Like a safe word, it's the signal for us to pull out of the op. If I so much as utter it, Quinn will get me out.

"Avery, it's highly unlikely we'll come face-to-face with the Alpha in there." He nods toward the Skylark. "We're just playing a role. Gathering intel."

I nod once, and then our door is opened. Carson steps out, mimicking Larkin as he reaches in to take my hand. I allow him to pull me from the limo and I do as instructed, acknowledging Carson as my Master. I bow my head and walk behind him.

Keeping Carson's reassurance tucked close, I put one strappy heel in front of the other. The Alpha won't reveal himself here. No, like all filth that dwells below the radar, the Alpha will watch the transactions from afar, until he's assured the deals are complete. Then, his accomplices will lead us right to the bastard.

That's when the second half of our party will take over the operation. Quinn fears my part, but going into The Firm is far less dangerous than his job. An ache fills my chest. I trust him, and I trust that he's the best—he'll be safe.

The foyer of the hotel smells of gardenias, the flowers displayed in tall vases throughout the pristine entry. I keep my head bowed as we enter an elevator, and as soon as Larkin opens the panel to select the penthouse floor, the car bounds upward. My stomach tingles from the sudden motion.

"Here." Alexis turns toward me and presents a black satin mask. It's been deliberately selected because it covers most of my face. As she slips it over my head and arranges it on my eyes, she leans in close and whispers into the ear without the earpiece. "Don't be ashamed if you discover you enjoy being possessed. Only be ashamed if you deny yourself a chance to explore this side of yourself."

My heart thunders to life, and I'm intently focused on my breathing. She pulls away and drags my hair over my shoulders, looking me over. "There. Now you're ready."

I'm not given another second to ponder her words as the elevator doors open to the penthouse. I'm thrust forward on sheer exhilaration, adrenaline blistering my veins, as I somehow find the courage to step forward.

Low, bass-filled music pulses within the room. The beat strikes my chest at the same time my senses are assaulted with every other sensation. The flicker of candles, the scent of floral incense. It's impossible to keep my head bowed when I'm so tempted to look around.

From what I can discern, it's not crowded; Larkin and Alexis stated it wouldn't be—that these are not the masked faces of the regular members. These are the meticulously vetted and chosen buyers for the auction. The Alpha's special selection.

Which means these are some of the most vile, corrupt men

in all of the Virginia and DC area, if not the world. I wonder how many are politicians.

The walls are painted a deep red and black. Sheer material is draped between lounging spaces. Thick beams further separate the sections. And along the walls, bondage gear. Ropes. Chains. Toys. A room decorated to cater to any BDSM fantasy.

I stay a foot behind Carson as we weave through the throng gathered in the middle. I can't help it; I peek up to witness Larkin step onto a platform and lift his hands to quiet the chatter before I stare back down at the lacquered floor.

He's donned a mask, as well as Alexis, who stands just below him. Every person here wears some form of cover to conceal his or her identity. It won't matter. That won't protect them. Every single body in this penthouse is, as I stand here, being identified and marked by Quinn and Sadie in the surveillance room set up at Lark and Gannet.

The list of names Larkin gave Quinn of the buyers was the trade-off for our cooperation on this operation.

"Sirs and madams," Larkin says, and the room quiets further to hear his speech. "I welcome you to the first ever Firm Auction." Light applause trickles through the room. Carson only hesitates a moment before he joins in. "Before the auction begins, please indulge in the festivities we've arranged for this evening. It's never ideal to purchase on impulse, so fill your gluttonous desires." A short burst of laughter erupts. "Enjoy."

Pressure beats at my temples. This is our cue to move to the voyeur section. Even though I've been prepped, the knowledge of what's about to commence jacks my heart rate.

Carson slips his arm through mine and guides me toward the lounging area. Larkin made sure we understood the dynamics of the penthouse, and we ease into the scene without garnering any unwanted attention.

I let Carson seat me on a spacious velvet couch, relieved to be in the safest area of the penthouse. So far, everything has gone according to plan. As Carson takes his spot beside me, accepting a flute of champagne from a hostess serving drinks, the room becomes a living force.

The music heightens, the lights dim, and from the other side of the room, in walks the most beautiful, exotic women I've ever seen. They're clad only in silver masks. Their gorgeous, naked bodies shimmer with a metallic gloss, illuminating their skin and plunging this scene into an ethereal realm.

Each woman takes up a post near one of the suited men. I've counted around ten men—buyers—so far. Some have brought their subs or slaves…or maybe even their wives along with them. I'm not sure how this works, what the parameters are—how one goes about purchasing another human being. But I don't have time to speculate as one of the breathtaking vixens approaches us.

I can almost hear Carson gulp his champagne as she stops right in front of him.

"Hello, Master. My name is Tanja." Her voice is a tinkle

soft chime. "I'm your gift tonight. How can I service you?"

We, however, were not warned about this development. And for all Carson's coaching, he's barely able to keep his stoic expression in place. I spot Larkin near the platform, and he raises his champagne glass in our direction. A knowing smile spreads across his face. *Bastard.*

Carson clears his throat, sets the flute on the floor to his right. "My angel and I like to watch," he says, pressing back into the couch. "That is, of course, why we're in the voyeurs' section."

Her smile sets her soft features aglow behind the mask. "Your wish is my command, Master." She beckons with a curl of her finger, and another woman saunters over from across the room. She's trailed by a tall, leanly built man in a black suit. My chest constricts. This was not a part of the program. And what's worse, despite his mask, I recognize him as Larkin's named partner. Mike Gannet.

Gannet inclines his head to us in greeting as he stretches out along the couch, then he waves his hand in a quick flick to the women. "Give us a show," he orders. Then to Carson, he leans his head near and says, "I can rarely bring myself to share my sub—" his dark eyes devour the blonde "—but when in Rome, right?" He turns a jeering smile on Carson, but his hungry gaze flits to me.

A shiver crawls along my skin. I focus on keeping my gaze sealed on the women as they begin to fondle and caress. The blonde, Gannet's sub, adorns the same diamond encrusted bird pendant around her neck I've seen on Alexis.

"She belongs to me," Carson says, a dark note in his voice. "I don't share. Ever."

He's been instructed well on how to handle this particular situation. But, I don't think we took the partners into consideration when formulating this tactic. I tug at my collar, and remembering the camera, force my hand to my lap.

"I see," Gannet says, returning his attention to the two women who are aggressively touching and kissing... "However, for this special event, we've all had to make a few sacrifices, you see. I strongly encourage you to play by the rules and allow your beauty to explore the festivities."

A hint of familiarity barbs my mind. Alexis said a similar thing to me in the elevator and now, Gannet's warning rings clear. Carson and I don't belong. We sure as hell don't understand the rules. Was Alexis forewarning me? If so, why be so cryptic?

Panic threads my spine as I gather my nerve. I lower my gaze and face Carson. "If it will please you, Master."

Gannet laughs. "Oh, unleash the girl. Let her play. I assure you, you'll be greatly rewarded for your trust." His eyes narrow on Carson.

A hiss of static sounds in my ear. "Carson, Avery's right. You're being tested," Sadie says. "Order Avery to join in—but not to undress. It's the only way to compromise and show your gratitude for being selected to the partners."

Carson bends forward and picks up his flute. He takes a

long swig before he sets it back down. "I find myself feeling rather grateful this evening," he says to Gannet. "And of course, I'm inclined to show that gratitude."

"All right. Good," Sadie encourages, then the link cuts off, silent once again.

"Salina," Carson addresses me by my crafted identity. "Stand and join Tanja and Gannet's lovely morsel in some entertaining play for us all." He reaches over and grasps my chin, forcing my gaze to meet his. "But, you will not remove your dress."

As much as I've been coached, it's still difficult to enact this role. I swallow, knowing my nerves are at least helping me appear the demur and devout submissive I've been prepped to be. "Yes, Master."

I can do this. I control my body. No one is taking, no one is forcing. Mindset is everything. Gannet is not Wells. These men—though as vile as they are—are not Wells. I continue to mentally prepare myself as I stand.

The full scenic view impacts me, and my breath stutters. Debauchery at its finest fills the penthouse. It's a shock to my system, but it's not appalling. There's a delicate texture threading the air, vibrating, tantalizing. And once I accept this fiction, I slip into the character of Salina willingly.

Two sections over, a couple has sex openly on top of a table. The man thrusts into the bronzed woman unguarded, uninhibited. All around me hands paw and eyes watch. The sharp *whip* of leather meets flesh, stinging the air. It ignites my senses, and when Tanja presses her body against mine, my skin blazes.

I don't look at Carson as her hands roam along my hips, down to my thighs, though I can feel his eyes on me. And I know this is part of the mission. But I desperately wish he'd look away as the naked woman behind me suddenly kisses my neck.

"Not on the mouth, Lila," Gannet chastises his sub. "I have my rules, too." He directs this comment to Carson, and then I'm acutely aware of both men watching the scene unfold before them.

Tanja tugs at my satin dress, yanking it up my thigh. I let my hands caress her, feeling the silken, glittery oil coating her skin. I close my eyes, but that doesn't prevent the others from seeing me on the monitors.

Quinn.

He's watching me through Carson's camera.

The thought comes as a swift kick to my chest, awakening my trance. I could almost lose myself in this moment, allowing a dull glaze to coat my mind and feel removed. Or I could do as Alexis suggested: explore. Only the reality of my feelings for Quinn won't let either happen.

I belong to Quinn.

"Your skin is so soft," Tanja whispers in my ear, her tongue tasting my lobe. She positions my thigh against her hip, and I grip her shoulders, seeking balance. My foot finds purchase on the low marble table. "It's too bad your Master won't let you remove this." She fondles the shoulder clasp of my dress. "But we can work around that."

The clasp comes loose and the strap slips down. My dress falls open, revealing my breast. "Oops," she says, a deviant smile playing at her mouth.

Gannet's boisterous laugh spears me, and the shock of the girl's yelp as he swats her ass covers my alarm. I snatch my strap and hastily refasten the clasp.

"Can never train them completely," Gannet remarks to Carson. "They love seeking punishments." But really, he's not put out at all by this. Rather, he looks delighted the woman tested Carson's authority.

Tanja wears a sultry pout on her lips, but she's quick to move on, her fingers delicately kneading their way up my inner thigh as Lila pulls my shoulders back, reclining me against her chest. I feel the press of her nipples through the sheer satin material, then I'm jolted by the shock of Tanja's fingers slipping my thong aside.

She doesn't stop there, and soon she's pushing her slim fingers inside me while the other woman caresses my breasts. My whole body thrums with tension, and it's impossible to relax. I'm going to blow this. They're going to see right through me...

"Don't you fucking look away," Quinn's voice snaps in my ear.

I startle, my gaze shoots to Carson—who is staring at the floor. He bends over to grab his champagne and whispers into his mic, "I can't watch this. I can't watch Avery—"

"You're going to get her hurt," Quinn cuts in, his voice thick, grating. "Look at her, or I'll beat the shit—"

"Ten minutes until the auction commences, gentlemen." It's Larkin's voice traveling through the penthouse, the announcement breaking into the feed. Relief is a wave crashing into me.

"Well, then," Gannet says. "Sorry to cut the show short, but my sub must tend to her Master now."

Furthering my relief, the blonde is suddenly gone. Gannet leads her by the wrist to the couch, and my bated breath springs free.

Tanja pushes her mouth into another pout. "My time is up." She turns to Carson and bows. "Are you sure I can be of no more service to you, Master?"

But it's Gannet who answers. "You can be of service to me." He grasps her by the waist and hauls her over the couch, kicking her ass up toward him. He winks at Carson as he unbuckles his belt. "It's not good to peruse the menu on an empty stomach, right?" He quotes Larkin's speech with a slick smile slanting his mouth. "We all know the merchandise isn't as fulfilling when we get it home." He nods toward me. "Eat. Drink. Satisfy your urges so you make a wise purchase, my friend."

My eyes flick to Carson as Gannet proceeds to take Tanja right there. He's doing a terrible job of masking his shock. This is not happening. I lower my foot from the table and slowly approach Carson, moving at a glacier's pace. Waiting for Sadie or Colton or Quinn or God, even Jefferson, to come back with instructions on how to get out of this.

Finally, Sadie says, "Just fake it."

I almost open my mouth to retort, a derisive laugh caught in my throat. *Fake it.*

Fucking seriously?

A quick sweep around the room captures the very *not* faking it happening all around us. "They're all caught up in the moment," Sadie continues. "It's dark. Just go with the motions."

Carson gives me a sure nod. "Come here," he orders, sounding authoritative and much more confident than I feel.

I watch as he eases his hips up and unbuckles his belt. He tugs his pants down just enough to reveal the blue boxer briefs beneath. He leaves those in place. Collecting what courage I have left, I hike my dress and straddle him without a second thought.

His hand grasps the back of my neck and he brings me forward, resting my cheek against his. "Say the word, and we're out," he whispers.

I can't lie, as Gannet thrusts and grunts practically inches from me, brutally slamming his hips against Tanja as the blonde sucks on her breasts... *Lemon* is right on the tip of my tongue, ready to be spat out to end this humiliation.

But those women. The victims.

The ones waiting behind the scenes to be sold.

I'll never be able to look at myself in the mirror without

hating what I see if I don't go through with this. My actions in correcting the drug have sealed their fate to become a mindless, doped slave…and now, I can save them.

"We've come too far," I whisper in his ear as I undulate my hips, forcing all self-doubt to the back of my mind.

"All right," Carson says, doing his best to follow my lead. "Just don't say *come* again."

A clatter sounds through my earpiece before the connection goes silent, and I just know it's Quinn—I can feel him on the other side. Shit.

As I lift up, I see it on Carson's face; the fear of Quinn throttling him in his pinched eyes. I'm starting to feel bad for the guy. He's here risking his life and career right along with the rest of us, and yet, he can't win in this scenario.

Either we fail and he loses everything, or we succeed…and Quinn rips him a new one. I'll make sure to intercept Quinn before that happens.

I catch Carson's gaze and nod, urging him to stay focused on me. At this point, we're the prudes. The damn prudish couple amid a sea of wicked, scandalous sex and sin. And we stick out like it.

Taking the initiative, I ride Carson harder, faster, rocking my hips. I brace my hands against the couch and throw my head back, and shit—the clasp on my dress gives. The cool sensation of air greets my skin, and I'm only thankful for the dim lighting.

When I look down at Carson, he's staring at my stomach.

I grab Carson's hands and bring them to my breasts. We're adults. They're just boobs. We have to do something—*anything* to make this believable.

And I guess it's starting to work, because I feel Carson becoming aroused, growing hard beneath me. There's an apology in his eyes, and I place my finger over his mouth to stop him from voicing it. Hell, there's people all over having intense, right-out-of-a-porno sex. I don't fault him for being turned on.

For the first time, I'm not ashamed I have trouble in that department. Grinding against Carson doesn't do it for me. Quinn has been the only person to excite me since I escaped my dungeon. Carson, however, doesn't suffer my defect, and that's clear as he becomes bold and takes over the perusal of my breasts.

He pinches my nipples and thrusts his hips upward, grinding himself against me. "Jesus," he hisses, then attempts to suppress a harsh groan.

"Kiss me," he says, and my eyes go wide. "Kiss me and this will be over."

One of his hands slips along the back of my neck, his fingers spearing into my hair, as he pulls me to him. His lips smash against mine, the impact nearly as stunning as the feel of his other hand sliding beneath my dress and seeking my ass. His fingers skim my sex and press against the fabric of my underwear...and then I feel his erection pulsing against me.

Carson's groan almost cancels out the blistering roar that

crackles through the feed.

Quinn's shout jars us apart as the lights blink on. I pull my dress up and secure the strap over my shoulder. Then I press my mouth against his ear. "Quinn's going to kill you."

Before I can move away, he holds me there. "I know. And I'm sorry, but that was the sexiest lap dance ever, and I couldn't help myself."

I cut my eyes at him as I slip off his lap and adjust my dress. God knows this means nothing in the grand scheme of things. I've had to accept circumstances I never wanted to before. One of them being that our bodies react to stimuli even when our brains protest. I know this because Wells forced my body to deceive me despite my own will.

But my sympathy for Carson's precarious situation dissolved the moment his tongue pushed inside my mouth and his fingers stole a cheap grope. If I tell that to Quinn... Well, Carson would pretty much be a dead man walking.

Gannet situates himself as the women toddle off to clean up. A disgusted feeling assaults my stomach, but luckily my attention is diverted as Larkin's voice sounds out loud and clear.

"And now, gentlemen, the main attraction." The lights dim again, and one center spotlight winks on to showcase the platform. "All sales are finalized at the end of the auction. No returns, no trades. Let the bidding begin."

A large monitor descends from the ceiling above the stage, and I stumble back against the couch. Carson helps me find my seat. My heart lurches and threatens to burst through my chest wall at the sight of a young woman appearing on the screen.

She only wears a black bra and underwear. A black bag covers her head. But I recognize the fresh mark on her upper thigh immediately. She's been branded by the Alpha.

My breath halts. My back goes taut. The man holding her arm dons a black ski mask. He yanks the bag from her head and lifts her chin, showing her off for the men in this room. My fingers ache as they dig into the velvet.

This is why we're here. This is why we're sacrificing everything.

CHAPTER 16

BOMBSHELL

QUINN

My blood boils, my knuckles along my right hand sting with fresh scrapes. I sink my hands under the cool stream and splash my face. The bite of cold water defuses some of the heat simmering beneath my skin.

"Are you ready yet?"

I glance in the mirror. Colton stands behind me in the bathroom, arms crossed, eyes assessing. "Almost," I grit out.

He and Jefferson wrestled me out of the conference room before I could threaten that fucking shit Carson. Seeing Avery gyrating on top of him...his hands touching her...her mouth on his... My vision flares red.

I lost my shit and took my frustration out on a wall. Larkin now has a couple holes in the drywall of his conference room. It's fucking stupid, I know. This is the op; this is the job. And

I'm a grown fucking man who knows the difference, but that doesn't stop the seething anger from raging anew.

I slam down the tap and let the water drip from my face.

"I get it," Colton says. "If it was Sadie in there, I'd probably have Carson's prick on a platter before morning." He takes a step closer. "But he was doing his job, keeping Avery safe, by any means necessary. And Avery's suffered enough. She's been through enough. She doesn't need anyone else making what she had to do tonight any harder on her."

Fucking hell. I glare at him in the mirror. I'm not hearing this from Rope Boy right now. "My patience is through." I turn and head toward the door. "I'm not discussing my relationship with Avery with you."

"Yeah, not now," he says. "But maybe you should later."

I stop. Stand at the door, fists clenched.

"Who else do you have to talk to?" he asks. "Really talk to. Who will understand what Avery's been through, how that effects the both of you."

I swipe my hands over my face. As much as I loathe the guy, he makes a valid point. "But this isn't happening now." I look over at him.

He nods. "Let's get her out of this safely, then. So it *will* happen."

With that said, we head back into the surveillance hub. Sadie is seated before the monitor, her eyes fixed on a screen within the screen. "They've brought out the first girl."

And like that, my focus is where it needs to be. I pull up

165

my chair beside hers. "Do we know how many girls yet?"

She shakes her head. "We knew they wouldn't be able to sneak them into the hotel. Too risky. They're transmitting the feed from somewhere in the city, though. I just can't narrow down the location." She switches to another monitor that shows the signal bouncing around the city. "It's practically pinging every tower."

I exhale heavily. "Jefferson, take over tracing the signal."

"On it." He moves into position and intercepts the keyboard. Turns out, the driver has some skills to come in handy, after all.

"Bonds, zoom in on the screen. See if you can clear up the image." I squint at the monitor. "It's dark, but looks like a warehouse. There's a roll door in the background."

"Might be the same place Avery was taken to," Sadie says, and I glimpse the worry in her eyes.

If all goes to plan, it's where Avery's about to be taken again. Dammit. I hate it, but Colton's right. Avery is the strong one here. She didn't have to do this, and yet, she was the first to step forward.

I ease back in my chair and bring out the picture from my inseam pocket. Avery's dark eyes and bright smile. A picture capturing a moment in time when Avery knew nothing of suffering and pain—not like she does now.

A deep ache burrows beneath my chest. That woman still exists somewhere below all her pain, and she's desperately trying to find her again. Avery's putting herself on the line, risking it all, in order to end the threat and bring herself back.

None of this is black and white. There's no right or wrong. In this world, there are only people who cause pain, and the recipients of that pain. Avery was swept into a dark storm, unaware, and she's been treading the downpour ever since.

I wanted to be her hero. But she's the hero of her own story. Even heroes make mistakes.

And now, she's putting herself in danger to correct them.

"Wait—what's that?" Sadie zeros in on the masked man restraining the girl. She's shivering and crying, and where Sadie enlarges the angle, I see a syringe in his hand.

Shit. I swivel my chair around to face Colton. "Earpiece?"

His eyebrows hike. "I guess it's safe to give it back to you now." He digs into his pocket and produces the earbud he jacked when I lost control. Maybe it's best he did. Once this is over, I don't want the memory of Carson's hands on Avery…or anything else that transpired.

It's already going to be hard enough to curb the impulse to break Carson's face every time I see him.

I stuff the bud into my ear just as a high-pitched whine bleeds into our feed. We rear back from the feedback. Then, a deep, garbled voice booms from the main speakers.

"Thank you for joining me this evening."

Sadie and I exchange glances. "The Alpha," we nearly say in unison.

"We're still recording?" I ask.

She confirms before the distorted voice continues. "I pride

167

myself that this is much more than the average auction, and I'm prepared to demonstrate this fact."

On the monitor, the masked man raises the syringe and inserts the needle into the thrashing woman's arm. Within seconds, she's calm. Docile. Accepting her predicament. My stomach roils with vitriol at the display.

"Trifecta, gentlemen," the Alpha says. "With every purchase tonight, you'll receive a sample, and the means to set up a year's supply of this revolutionary drug that's going to change the industry."

The camera pans closer to the woman, deliberately highlighting her rapid-changing demeanor. I've seen this before. I experienced it with Avery. And fuck—I want nothing more than to punch through the monitor and rip the Alpha's throat out.

The woman touches herself, her moan sounding pained. She grinds against the masked man and claws at his jacket. She strips her panties away and begins gratifying herself...

I look away.

"What would you pay to own a never-sated slave? Hungry for you every second of the day?" The Alpha pauses for a beat. "As you can see, a drug in such demand couldn't possibly have a price tag. It's simply priceless. But everything *must* have a price. Choose yours."

Then the Alpha's robotic voice fades out, and all that remains is a victimized woman on the screen.

Immediately, the buyers start to bid. Below the projection

screen, an underscored box lights up with numbers rapidly ascending into the thousands.

"Hell." Sadie's breathless curse conveys exactly what we're witnessing. Hell.

And that's precisely where we're going to send the Alpha.

After the initial purchase of the first woman, the auction moves along quickly, and at the very least, no other woman has to suffer the Trifecta demonstration she endured.

"Larkin's giving Carson the go-ahead to place a bid on the fourth girl," Sadie says, pressing her finger to her earpiece.

Larkin's voice comes in over the feed. "Bid now," he tells Carson. On the monitor, through Alexis's camera, we watch Carson push a button on the table before him.

Carson just needs to purchase one girl for us to be in. And he needs to do it without raising any alarms. The Alpha used Lark and Gannet's resources to vet the buyers, and we built an identity for Carson based on facts—but we indulged upon those facts. Carson being the department leak actually did work in our favor.

Now, all he has to do is keep his cool and place the winning bid, and the Alpha will be within our reach.

"The man to his left—" Sadie checks her tablet with the list of buyers already identified "—Judge Ramos is putting up a fight for this girl." She glances at me. "Is it believable that Carson can actually afford a hundred grand?"

That's what the bid is about to reach. "Yeah, it is," I say. "Larkin transferred just over that into his account today. Made it look like a series of deposits over the past year." I shake my head. "Looks like being a weasily leak pays off."

Sadie releases a clipped breath. "You're never going to let him live this down, are you?"

"What do you think?"

Her strained smile is a beacon amid the tension. And for just a moment, it feels like I have the old Sadie back—the profiler who grated on my nerves, but who I could always count on. Maybe that never changed. But when you uncover someone's darkest secrets, you just can't go back to the way things were.

"The judge is out," Sadie says as she focuses on the auction. "Carson's in at just over a hundred thousand. Holy shit."

Holy shit is right. Carson doesn't get to actually keep any of the money, and the actual transaction will never take place—but I'm sure he's feeling the pressure at having just bid away a small fortune.

"He stayed cool," Colton says. "Gotta be a difficult thing to pull off for a gambling addict." His gaze flicks to me, and yes—I get it. Everyone is being tested tonight.

Not just me.

"It appears they're moving into the finale," Larkin says into the feed. Three women are brought before the camera, the bags over their heads yanked away. We haven't been able to identify any of the women, but if we pull this off, not a single one of them will be sold.

After a short rundown on each of the girls' stats—virgin,

pure, blond, brunette—the masked man places his hand over the first girl's head, and the bids light up.

"Why are they suddenly rushing?" Sadie asks, looking at the monitor with the hopping transmitted signal.

"Someone else is tracing the signal," Jefferson says. "And whoever it is, isn't as stealthy as us. They must know."

Damn. But there's no time to route the attack. By the time the last girl is sold, the screen inside The Firm goes dark.

My back locks taut as we await the Alpha's next move. Come on. *Come on.*

Larkin moves onto the platform, and my jaw sets, every muscle corded tight. "Gentlemen, that concludes the auction." Five men wearing black ski masks appear from the other side of the penthouse and stand at the platform.

My lungs refuse to take a breath.

"Please remain seated as our friends here distribute your buyer cards with generated purchases," Larkin says.

"Trackers going out," Sadie confirms, checking the signal.

Each card has a transmitter chip that we'll use to track. It was a stipulation of the Alpha, which Larkin and I decided to exploit. Using his own system against him.

"Once you have your card, please head toward the elevator," Larkin instructs. "You'll now be paired in groups, and each group will have one of these fine gentlemen escort you to the pick-up location for your purchase."

That's our cue. We're up and collecting our gear as Larkin disappears behind the screen.

"I've done my part," Larkin whispers to us. "Good luck."

His connection is terminated.

I stare at the monitor, my chest tight as I watch Avery prepare to go dark.

"Avery," I say. "It's almost over. Stay strong. I'm right behind you."

She can't respond, but she touches her left arm, giving me her signal that she's all right. The tension coiling my body releases just a bit, then I watch her stealthily remove the earbud and tuck it between the cushions of the couch before she follows Carson toward the elevator.

As we suspected, the masked men begin an inspection of the buyers, making sure they're clear of any weapons and recording devices, like phones. Carson and Avery pass inspection, but that means they're going into the next stage blind.

We all are. I no longer have a link to Avery.

"Jefferson, stay here and keep on that signal," I say. "Just in case—"

He confirms before I complete my thought. *Just in case we lose them.* That isn't an option. We all know at any point, the Alpha could change gears, have the buyers toss the cards, switch course. But we just need to be headed in the right direction…

"We're ready." Sadie's gaze captures mine, a hint of a question there.

"Ready," I answer.

We're ready to go in and pull off the biggest bust I've ever been a part of with only three officers of the law and one civilian.

But it's what's on the line that assures we will succeed.

Carson and Avery are traveling to the pick-up destination with Judge Ramos and the CEO of a software company. And their chauffeur, one of the masked cronies.

I drive while Sadie tracks their movement through the outskirts of Arlington on her tablet.

"They're slowing," she says, and I pull back. "Just keep at a steady speed until I confirm they've turned."

After a few tense moments, she directs me onto a road leading toward an abandoned warehouse. My hands slick against the steering wheel, my adrenaline climbs.

"We get Avery out before—"

"We will," Sadie assures. "Don't worry, Quinn. Carson knows the drill. He'll have her out of harms way first."

A flashback of the mission to rescue Avery from the sailboat barrels to the front of my mind. The waiting, my insides sick with anxiety every torturous second that passed. The pressure building right before we went in. The fear of not finding her alive…

I drive the thoughts away. She's not a hostage. She's a part of the mission, and she's strong. She was strong then, and she's even stronger now.

And then there's no more time for reflection as I glimpse a blacked out warehouse up ahead. No one talks. We've gone over the plan—over and over. We *all* know the drill.

There's only one aspect of this operation that remains undecided.

Whether it will be me or Sadie that pulls the trigger to take out the Alpha.

I have a feeling she's going to move first. Some kind of vigilante bullshit where she presumes she'll be protecting me—keeping me from committing an act that will haunt me for years to come.

I've wrestled with this very thing. If there's no imminent threat—can I kill in cold blood?

Avery's picture is virtually burned into my retinas, I've stared at it so long. I need to see that carefree woman once again. I want to be the one who makes her safe.

Imminent threat: I guess that's defined by the person who's being threatened.

Avery will never be safe if the Alpha lives.

His connections run too deep, his reach extends too far. We're operating below the department's radar because we don't even know how far that reach goes. How high up.

I've made my choice. I made it the first night I held Avery's hand in the hospital.

She's mine to protect.

I park in a heavily shrouded section of the gravel parking

lot. The cars that transported the buyers here from the Skylark are parked up close, the buyers already inside the warehouse.

I unclip my holster and pull my gun free, then unlock the safety. I hear the decocker click to my right, Sadie prepared. She turns around to see Colton doing the same.

An unspoken countdown commences, and we exit the car on the beat of three and jog toward the warehouse.

The trill of crickets and brush of wind through the pines are the only sounds accompanying us as we advance. Once we're in place, backs to the building, the faint muffle of voices bleeds through the metal wall.

The side roll door has been left open, and I motion in that direction. I lead us around the building, conscious of the gravel with each step. We stop every few feet and listen. Then proceed.

Halting near the metal beam of the roll door, I raise my hand, hold it steady, waiting for Carson's signal.

The low voices inside die down, the warehouse stills. A creak of a door, then the distinct, distorted voice we heard during the auction. Carson doesn't have to warn us; the Alpha is here.

I drop my hand.

We rush in.

There's an ephemeral moment of dread, suspending time around me in a morbid limbo, until I lock on to Carson rushing Avery toward the side of the warehouse. Fractions of a second. Those split atoms of time can last an agonizing eternity.

I breathe. Time speeds up. Instinct kicks in.

I shout, "Hands in the air!"

My voice ricochets around the building. The echo bounces back at me before the chaos hits. "On the ground! On the ground!"

Several of the civilian buyers hit the floor, the others break out into a run. I drop to the floor. Sadie and Colton follow suit and hit the ground as the first bullet rings out.

I sight my gun on the perp opening fire and pull the trigger, taking out his calf. He drops and grabs his leg. I'm already locking on to the next perp before his scream recoils against the gunfire.

"Stop!"

And just as suddenly as the shooting began, it ends. The masked men pull back their weapons. My breathing ragged, I try to steady my breaths so I can hear past the ringing in my ears.

I scan the back of the warehouse and quickly assess the numbers. Nine suited men scattered against the ground and side of the warehouse. Four masked men: three standing guard around seven huddled women, one wounded on the floor. Carson and Avery are safely out of sight. Then one shadowed figure steps forward.

"Freeze!" I shout.

The person halts, but only a moment before they leisurely progress closer. "I'm unarmed," he says. The voice is no longer obscure. "I'm sure we can work this out without any more bloodshed."

"Tell your men to drop their weapons and kick them forward," I order.

The man steps into the beam of moonlight streaming from outside. "You heard the officer," he says. "Lower your weapons and kick them forward."

His men do on command. The clatter of guns hitting the floor all in unison sets my jaw. As soon as the weapons are out of reach, I glance behind me, taking Sadie and Colton into account. They're uninjured.

I get to one knee, keeping my gun aimed on the man in a black suit, and then rise to my feet. "You're in charge of this operation?"

Hands held aloft, he maintains the smirk on his face. A face I've never seen before, but that could be any face in a crowd. His black hair is slicked back, neatly cropped. His gold jewelry glints in the moonlight. His smooth features denote youth, but he shows no fear of the gun pointed at his head.

"I am," he says, his voice dropping low. "And I assume you're the one in charge of your operation—" he nods to the three of us "—and I assume because you're not backed by a task force or the FBI, then you've come here as part of your own agenda."

My hand grips the gun tighter. My finger braced over the trigger.

I hear the decock of a gun; a bullet chambered. The *click* resounds loudly in the still room. It's not my gun; it's Sadie's.

177

Now or never. If I don't pull the trigger, she will.

"No argument there, I see." He tilts his head. "So tell me, what do you want? Money? Women?" He looks over his shoulder at the girls before finding my gaze again. "Advancement in your career. Name it. I promise, I can make it happen."

There's only one way for him to give me what I want. I curl my finger over the trigger…

"I want your name," I demand.

His dark eyes stare into mine. "I go by many." A smile lights his face. "You won't find Dorian McGregor on any of your wanted lists, but it's the one I choose to go by most often. I promise, I'm a man of my word. Anything you want, I can make happen. Name your price."

I don't blink. I look him right in his eyes as I squeeze…

"Lower the weapon!"

My finger halts mid-pull, my hand trembles with restraint, and I know this is my last chance—

"I said, lower the gun, Detective Quinn." I recognize the voice. In my peripheral, I spot Agent Bell moving into the center of the warehouse.

The sound of booted feet trampling the scene reverberates through the building as the Feds raid the warehouse. A ruckus of shouts and collection of weapons and apprehending the masked men…all while I still have my sight laser-focused on the Alpha.

"Quinn." Her voice is steady, calm. "You're better than this.

It's over. Lower your gun and let's bring him in. The right way."

I release the trigger and pull back my gun. A searing breath grips my lungs as I suck it down. Then I force my eyes away from the Alpha. I look at Special Agent Bell as the Alpha is taken to the ground and handcuffed.

"You used me," I say to her. "You used my department."

Her eyes widen with a hint of remorse, but I doubt she feels any at all. Her career is made. She gets the fame of bringing down the head of a criminal network.

She sighs as she reaches into her jacket pocket and brings out the phone she gave me. "I wasn't sure if you'd put together a side op or not," she says. "But when I tracked the phone and discovered it stowed in one of the perp's vehicles…" She shrugs. "Good evasive tactic. You did have a couple of my agents chasing this phone around the city for a few hours."

I'd hoped for longer than a few. I had Carson dump the phone in one of the perp's cars our uniforms were tailing. It was reasonable to believe that I'd keep close watch over the two perps who we busted in the body transport van. Eventually, they might've led us to the Alpha.

But we didn't have time to wait.

I just needed Bell and the Feds off my case and away from Lark and Gannet.

"So it was the Feds hacking the transmitted auction signal." I holster my gun. "You could've gotten someone hurt, or killed. You almost blew the whole thing."

Bell turns to watch the agents begin reciting the buyers

179

their rights, then she swings her gaze to me. "Guilty as charged. You're not the only one with inside intel, detective. I've had my eye on McGregor for a while. The tip about the auction came from a protected source."

She steps closer. "We had it covered. No one was in immediate danger. I know somewhere deep down, you knew the right thing to do was to call me. And even though you never did…subconsciously, you wanted it to happen this way."

I shake my head. I fucking hate psychobabble bullshit. "I think the phone taking a scenic tour around town speaks for itself. You should've been transparent with my department on who you were investigating from the start."

She raises her eyebrows in mock indignity. "You want to talk transparency? After I find you here with only two for backup?" Her dark eyes drill through me. "Just what was the plan, Quinn? Would you have pulled that trigger?"

I don't avert my eyes, but I don't give her an answer. I'm not sure I have one.

She rubs her forehead. "No, you're right. We should've trusted each other enough to work together. This could've gone bad. It didn't…but next time, we really should work together."

Next time.

Because the Alpha isn't dead.

Teeth clenched, I glance back at Sadie. "I don't want anyone else going down for this," I say. "It was my op. I put it together. My colleagues were only following my orders."

"You got it," she says, and I look at her, surprised. "You

were in charge of helping your department organize an op within the parameters of the FBI task force. That's how it will be reported."

Unbelievable. "And if it *had* gone bad?"

"Then—" she shrugs "—the FBI would've had no part of it, of course. You and your team would've been arrested for obstruction, and you would've probably lost your badge for good."

Fucking Feds. "Fine. Then I'm done here."

"You'll thank me tomorrow, detective." She touches my arm gently. "When you sit behind your desk instead of the inside of a cell." My nostrils flare, and I move away from her touch. "Go home, Quinn. Sleep. Get some perspective. We'll take it from here."

Agent Bell starts to walk off, but then pivots around. She tucks the phone inside my pocket. "You still might need a friend. Or maybe I will one day." She winks and then sets off toward the Alpha. Dorian McGregor. Whoever he is, he's no longer my concern.

All I want this second is to take Avery away from here.

There's the matter of debriefing first, however. Making sure all parties are on the same page before we're released from the scene. When Agent Bell attempts to pull me into the questioning, I turn my back on her and head toward my car. I've heard enough. While the others are debriefed, I lean against the hood, arms crossed over my chest. I don't mind waiting alone.

181

Carson is the first to be released. Unfortunate for him. I push off the hood as he strides away from the group.

To his credit, he walks directly toward me, even though he should be running in the opposite direction. He does stop a good distance away, though. He definitely should do that. Smart bastard.

"I just wanted to say…" he starts, driving a hand through his hair. His whole body is tense. "What happened back there. In The Firm…I didn't mean—"

I step up to him and cup the back of his neck, bringing his head next to mine. "I owe you a dick punch. But it's not happening tonight." I pat him on the shoulder. Hard.

I want Carson sweating just when that punch is going to come for a good, long while.

"Avery's safe." My gaze wanders to where she and Sadie are wrapping up with Bell. "For now, that's all that matters. You protected her." I meet his eyes. "For that…thank you."

His shoulders deflate, the fear still evident but dissipating. "I'll take that punch like a man when it comes."

Yes, he will.

Once Bell releases the rest of our team from debriefing, they meet us at my car. Sadie still has an arm anchored around Avery, shielding her from the chaos.

I'm acutely jealous of that touch, that protection she's offering her, and I don't hesitate as I steal Avery away and wrap both arms around her, tucking her close to my body.

She shivers against me. "I still don't understand what

happened," she says.

I stare at Sadie from over the top of Avery's head. "We got made."

Sadie inhales a deep breath. "Not the first time the Feds swooped in to steal the show." But I see it in those green eyes; the doubt. The skepticism. The question she won't voice but is simmering—whether or not I actually informed Agent Bell.

She'll probably always wonder, always question if she can trust me—fully trust me now. I guess that makes us even, then.

"I'm taking Avery home." I gather her under my arm. "We'll lay low tomorrow. Let the Feds have their glory. Then, play it by ear. Discuss what we need to. No one makes a statement until then."

With a nod, Sadie gives me one last guarded look, then her and Colton climb into the back of the car. Carson follows them. Avery sits up front with me, and it's a tense drive back to the city, where we all allow each other the privacy of our own thoughts.

In a way, we succeeded. And we failed.

The true fallout of our actions lingers at the edge, where darkness and certainty still hang in the balance.

CHAPTER 17

CARNAL

AVERY

haven't yet processed the events of tonight. During the drive into the city, I purposely kept my thoughts void of the Alpha. Trying not to place him, to match his voice with the one I heard over the intercom in the warehouse lab. Not to picture his face beneath the plain white mask of the man who stuck me with a syringe and drugged me.

Not to feel the cold intrusion of steel from the gun inside me...

Was he any of them? It's hard to correlate the mastermind villain we thought him to be with the man—just a man—we brought down tonight.

Still, every single fragmented piece spins on a loop inside my head. A vicious, never ending circle, like a debilitating OCD trigger that will never be satisfied.

I still feel the press of Sadie's concerned, lingering look she gave me when Quinn dropped the rest of our team off at their cars in the Lark and Gannet parking lot. Her eyes said so much in that moment. She's aware I've revealed our secret to Quinn. Soon, I'll have to confess as much to her, reassuring her that she won't be prosecuted for Wells' murder.

But not tonight.

Tonight, I want to pretend the Alpha will go away forever, along with all of his accomplices. That his extortion of me poses no threat; the fingerprint on the victim's neck doesn't exist. The trafficked women will return to their homes and loving families. Quinn will look at me and only see the woman I am. Not the revenge-motivated victim I became. That somewhere below the fear I still am.

Quinn's quiet as he signals his blinker and takes a right onto his street.

"I think it's safe for me to go home now." My voice seems too loud in the small space of the car.

He pulls into his apartment complex and parks. Kills the engine. "Did you see me hesitate?" he asks.

Confusion pulls the corners of my mouth down. "What do you mean?"

He doesn't look at me as he removes his key from the ignition. His focus remains hard on the windshield, at something beyond. "Did you see me hesitate to pull the trigger?"

I swallow hard. "Yes," I answer.

"You're not completely safe, Avery. I had one job to do;

pull the fucking trigger to ensure the threat against you was eliminated." He looks at me then. "And I fucking hesitated."

With a trembling hand, I go to reach for him, but he pulls away to open the door. "Wait."

He stays.

God, but I just wanted to pretend for one night that this was over. I'm not stupid; I know the Alpha can get to me—can get to all of us—from behind prison walls. If he even goes to prison at all. He'll be out on bail by the morning, just like the two men who kidnapped me.

It's never going to be over.

For just one night…I wanted to feel safe. I need to feel safe.

My admission rushes out. "I hesitated, too," I admit. "I had one job to do to make sure no one questioned Wells' death. To make it look like an accident, and I couldn't…" I trail off, the thick lump in my throat choking me off.

Quinn turns around. "The truth," he demands. "Not some bogus confession you wrote out of wanting to protect Sadie. Tell me the truth."

I swallow down my nerves. "I was there, but I didn't plant the evidence. I tried…but I'm just too weak."

"Get out of the car."

I blink rapidly. "What?"

He says nothing else as he exits the car and storms around to my side. He wrenches the door open and hoists me out of the seat before I can react.

Back braced against the car, I stare up into his face. The chill of the night air seeps past my thin dress, and I shiver. His gaze drags down my body. I flinch against his intense scrutiny, my insides no longer quaking from the cold.

"I can't feel my legs," I say. I'm trembling so badly now they can't sustain my weight.

With a low groan, Quinn bends at the knees and scoops me into his arms. "Can you feel your arms?" I can only nod. "Good," he says, kicking the door closed behind us. "Hold on, then."

He carries me across the lot and up the two flights of stairs to his apartment. The whole way, I keep my head buried in the pocket of warmth between his neck and chest. I memorize his scent. The feel of his strong arms cradling me.

If this moment is fleeting, I want to sear it into my memory.

Once he has the door open and we're inside his living room, I reluctantly lift my head and prepare to be put down. For his arms and his comforting scent to be taken away.

But he doesn't release me. He stalks straight to his bedroom, where he lays me on the bed and hovers from above. "I wanted to kill Carson tonight."

I blink up at him, my entire body aware, charged, by his proximity.

"I still might," he says, touching the clasp of my dress gingerly. "Seeing him touch you—" A muscle feathers along his clenched jaw. "I'm going to touch, kiss, possess every inch of your body. I'm going to erase the image I have of him with

187

you."

He's not asking permission. And I don't want him to. Maybe I missed some important shift where he moved past the fact that I'm a criminal. I should keep my mouth shut—but at the risk of ruining this moment, I have to know. "Aren't you disgusted by me? What I've been a part of – what I've done—?"

He answers me with a devastating kiss. His lips crush mine, stealing my breath and the rest of my demands. His weight bears down on me, his strong body a shield against my own destructive thoughts. He kisses me like he fears we don't have enough time; and maybe we don't. Tomorrow, anything could happen, so I latch on to him and kiss him back until my lips ache, competing with the deep pang in my chest.

His body covers mine, pressing me into the mattress, unrestrained and feral as he takes all of me within his kiss. He reaches down and grasps the back of my thigh, drags my leg up as he thrusts against me. I feel his want hard and demanding, the satin dress a poor barrier at disguising his desire.

"Carson had his hands on this dress," he says as he breaks away and grips the clasps. "His eyes... *All* their eyes on you..." He tears the dress down my body. The seams snap against the force.

I lie before him naked, all but my satin thong, unashamed. "I'm sorry if anything tonight hurt you—"

"Hurt? More like gutted. Ripped my fucking chest wide open." He presses his hand to my cheek, runs his thumb over my swollen lips. "But you have nothing to be sorry for."

188

I shake my head, and he lowers his face close to mine to hold me still. "Nothing to be sorry for," he repeats, emphasizing each word.

His meaning hits me hard. Understanding crashes into me at lightening speed.

"But I wanted Wells dead," I confess.

His chest rises with a forceful inhale. "I wanted to kill the Alpha." He roams his coarse hand along my leg, his gaze leisurely tracing its path up until his eyes capture mine. "But I didn't pull the trigger, and you didn't kill Wells, nor did you plant the evidence. I don't know if that makes us weaker...or stronger."

I definitely feel weaker. If it had been left solely up to me, I'd probably be in Price Wells' possession right now. Chained, tortured. Most likely dead. Yet I understand what Quinn is trying to say.

I reach up and cup his face. "It takes more strength to do the right thing."

His hazel eyes crease at the corners. "I'm not even sure I know what that is anymore."

"We'll figure it out."

I slip my fingers beneath the band of his slacks and grip his belt buckle, using it as leverage to pull myself up onto my knees. His breathing hitches as I lock an arm around his flexed shoulders, then proceed to loosen his belt.

I leave his buckle hanging open as I wander my hand up his taut stomach, undoing the buttons of his shirt as I go.

189

When I reach the top, I slip his tie free and drape it around my own neck, then I push his shirt off his shoulders, loving the feel of his warm flesh against my palms.

He allows me to pull his shirt off. Before he touches me again, I bring the shirt between us and fold the sleeves together. His brows draw together in confusion, but I continue to fold and then lay his shirt neatly on the edge of the bed.

"God, that's sexy." With one hand, he takes both ends of the tie and drags me to him, his mouth possessive over mine.

I want more, I want all of him, and I'm not ready when he breaks away.

"In The Firm…" He runs his hands up to my biceps, holding me at bay. "Were you aroused?"

A trace of a smile plays at my lips. "You mean, did I suddenly overcome my impaired libido with Carson?"

His nostrils flare, jaw clamped tight.

I push against his resistance, arching my chest toward his. "Dry as the Sahara. You're the only man who does it for me, Ethan."

Heat blazes in his eyes, his hands seal like bands around my arms as he pulls me hard to him. His mouth closes over mine, searing my lips with a branding kiss. This man lights me up like an inferno with only the slightest of touches, and now I'm frenzied, consumed under his primal swell.

His hand travels to my nape where he fists my hair, forcing me to bare the column of my neck to him. His hungry kisses scorch so perfectly. The abrasive feel of scruff along my skin sparks a fire, like a match striking flint against my flesh. "If I have any say about it—" warm breath whispers over my skin "—you'll never need that aphrodisiac concoction again."

Then we're both tugging at his slacks. Once he's discarded them, he pushes me back into the bedding, only giving me one heated look before flipping me onto my stomach. He bears down on top of me, his mouth attacking my flesh.

I grip at the comforter as he buries his hand in my hair, arching me into the perfect position to grind his hard cock against my ass. His other hand reaches between our bodies and snags the string of my thong. He tugs it up, fisting the satin until my clit throbs from the pressure.

A breathy moan slips free, and his carnal growl answers that plea. His fingers ease beneath my panties and seek the hot center pulsing for him. He swirls his fingers between my lips, gathering my wetness and hitting my clit just right. I buck against him, and his teeth nip at my ear, his heavy breaths erotic and stirring my desire.

"Spread your legs," he orders, but even as he says this, he's working my thighs apart with his knees.

The sudden *rip* of shredding material heightens my senses, the feel of his hands tearing my panties away deepens the ache in my core. The anticipation for Quinn to enter me is almost painful. My stomach muscles tense, the ache becoming unbearable.

He pulls the black tie still linked around my neck so that it aligns along my spine. He moves down my backside, lingering, massaging. Then he drives a hand under my pelvis and hikes my ass off the bed, his mouth taking me in the same beat. I release a moan at the feel of his tongue darting between my lips and tasting me.

His intense claiming tears at my control. As he takes me deeper, sucking my clit and sinking his tongue inside, my hips undulate to his rhythm, my spread-wide position making each time I thrust my pelvis a dirty act, and I become wetter.

His guttural groan against my flesh sends a jolt skittering over my skin. "More than once," he says, rearing back as he slaps his hand against my cheek and grips my skin. He forcefully pulls my back against his chest, both of us breathing fast. "I'll have you more than once tonight," he says just as he rests the tip of his cock at my entrance.

I reach behind and clutch his neck, bracing myself against him.

"Are you on—"

"Yes," I breathe out. "I'm on birth control, and if you don't fuck me right now I'm going to combust."

All the permission he needs, Quinn presses his hand against my pelvis and guides me down along this thick shaft. He sinks into me deep, to the hilt, spreading me and filling me all at once.

His groan travels the length of me, curling along my skin, vibrating against my ear. I feel powerful and helpless—an impossible stir of emotions. Desperate to own the strength in this man; desiring to be the one to bring him to his knees, battling with the insufferable desire to submit to him. Needing him to own me and take me in every way.

He backs out only to fill me again. His hips slam against me as I dig my nails into his neck, clinging to him the way his fingers brand my skin as he rocks into me harder each time.

As his thrusts overpower me, I search for purchase. His growl lashes through me as he wraps an arm around my middle and carries me to the head of the bed. I latch on to the headboard, then he's driving into me with unguarded thrusts, doing just as he promised; touching, kissing, possessing every inch of my body.

He's at my breast, fingers plucking my nipple until my insides are wound tight and begging for release. His other hand works my clit, sending erotic pulses of pleasure to every nerve ending, my body an over-strung instrument beckoning for the final strum to break me free.

And when I'm there—my moans unrestrained and his name falling liberally—he clasps onto my shoulders and drives his hips up, powerful thrusts slamming me, but I don't break.

Ethan Quinn is not gentle with me. He doesn't treat me like a delicate victim who may crack. He gives me exactly what I need, and he doesn't hold back. And as I meet him there, rocking my hips back into him with every thrust, he releases a harsh curse and pulls me away from the headboard.

It's the most intoxicating feeling; witnessing Quinn—who's always in control—lose every bit of his.

He falls across my body, burying himself inside me. His

arm hooks under my knee, and he brings my leg up to give him better access to drive as deep as he can—hitting the spot that makes me cry out over and over. I cling to his back, and when his mouth claims mine, his body becomes an unstoppable machine. My muscles gather, binding me with that delicious tension in my belly.

He pulls the tether free and I unfurl, an orgasm tearing through my being and slaying me.

"Jesus—" Quinn releases a string of expletives before his groan follows another long thrust. "You're fucking killing me…you're so fucking perfect." I feel my walls tighten around him just as he grows harder, causing me to clench, and then he sinks his teeth into my neck as his cock pulses deep within me.

I curl my fingers in his hair, my breathing labored. His own hot breaths caress my neck as he settles on top of me. His weight should be uncomfortable—but I crave it. I feel secure beneath him, safe and surrounded by his strength.

But Quinn is ever attentive, and he rolls me on top of him, wrapping his arms around the small of my back. I rest my head on his chest, listening to the rapid beat of his heart, his brisk breathing.

We lie like this for a while, until I'm nearly asleep, his light strokes along my back lulling me into a contented puddle atop him.

"I am in love with you. I should've said it before."

His admission awakens me. Quinn is not the type to give himself to another easily. I feel the depth of his love in the way he holds me. The way he protects me. He doesn't have to voice it, but I love the sound of his voice as he says the words. *I am in love with you.* "I'm in love with you."

He holds me tighter. "No one will ever hurt you again."

I lift up and prop my chin on his chest. "I'm always safe with you."

We're skirting all the things that really need to be said. What will happen when the Alpha is set free. When he fulfills his threat and exposes me; testing my loyalty to Sadie and to Quinn…when all I want is to protect both equally from any pain.

I guess those things are understood. We'll face them when we face them. But Quinn does ask one question before we allow the night to be our sanctuary once again.

"If it comes down to it—" his eyes stare into mine "—would you really take the blame for Wells?"

I don't want to think about what I'll lose when it's time to own my confession. But I'll never be able to live with myself if Sadie were punished for committing an act she only carried out to ensure that monster never hurt me or anyone else again.

"I would," I answer honestly. "Sadie did it for me. I owe her at least that much."

He accepts my answer with a kiss to my brow. His hand cups the back of my head as he places his lips to my forehead. Then there's very little talk between us; only the softly uttered avows in the dark as we devote the rest of our energy to touching and tangling, caressing and exploring each other.

195

Now that Quinn feels confident he's effectively claimed every inch of me, he spends the remaining hours of the night sealing that claim.

CHAPTER 18

WORTHY

QUINN

A n hour before the morning shift change, I'm inside the walls of the ACPD. I walk the hallways. Chug lukewarm, bitter coffee. Take note of every person.

By the time I reach the tech department, I'm sufficiently caffeinated and clearheaded. I awoke with a groggy sense of purpose this morning. And the harder I tried to ignore it, the more an idea took root, persistent in its hold over my mind.

It might've just been the aftereffects of passionate love making—and if ever confronted, I might even cop to that. More than enough good men have been brought down by their dicks. It's not the best excuse, but it's a believable one.

Only it's not the reason for why I pat Tommy on the shoulder and say, "Emily down in homicide said she has that thing ready for you."

At first, his face draws together in confusion, then he nods assuredly. "Oh, right. That thing. Damn." He glances around at his station. "I still have ten minutes to go before Rodney's in. I can't leave my station unmonitored."

It's a well known fact in the tech department that Tommy has it bad for Detective Emily. I don't know if she has any evidence for him to run or not, but it was worth a shot. Seems he'll take any morsel she offers him with high hopes. And with just the right push, I can send him running right to her.

"I got this," I say, smile tight. "I'm not on duty until six."

He glances around one more time, debating. "Are you sure you don't mind?"

"No. Go ahead before she leaves for the morning."

He's quick to take me up on my offer after that. Right there. The proof that even the best of men fall victim to their dicks.

Soon as he's gone, I check the time on my phone. There's a five minute delay in the security surveillance for the changeover. One small gap in the tech department when the cameras aren't recording. I discovered it while investigating Avery's abduction in the lab. And I'm using that blackout period...*now*.

I settle in behind his desk and pull up to the keyboard. The techs are still running a search on the print the crime lab sent up. Chances are, Price Wells won't turn up. I doubt he has a record, or is in any database across the country. He was meticulous. He covered himself every step of the way up until his last moments.

I could let it go. Let the print be logged as useless evidence. Fulfilling Wells' legacy, "UNKNOWN" stamped on the evidence label. But the Alpha didn't place his print on one of the vics just to torment Avery. He did so with the distinct purpose of keeping her under his thumb; to manipulate her; the threat to expose her ties to Wells always ready to be executed.

I didn't pull the trigger.

But I can sever the chain of evidence.

I locate the search and, with my hand hovering over the button, hit halt. I breathe through the tightness in my chest as I insert a USB drive and make quick work of erasing the print and replacing it with one I scanned from my department.

Ryland Maddox.

Turns out, Maddox had a few unpaid parking tickets back in college. He was brought in on a warrant back then and printed. He's also the Alpha's personal lawyer. The one who wormed his way into Lark and Gannet at the Alpha's bidding. He orchestrated the auction. He got the two perps who stole the van and kidnapped Avery out on bond, and he may even get them all the way off on that bogus claim with the support of the Alpha behind him. If anyone deserves to be tied to the Alpha Omega criminal network, it's him. I can live with that.

I once asked myself how far I would go to protect Avery.

I have my answer.

All the way if I have to.

Two partners at Lark and Gannet have proven to be corrupt. Wells and Maddox. There's a few more that need further investigation. Caleb Mason—who seems to have disappeared—Mike Gannet, and Chase Larkin.

Larkin gets a slight pass for now. I'll give him credit for stepping up to do the right thing. He helped stop the sell of trafficked sex slaves. I figure ridding Maddox from Larkin's law firm makes us about square.

But I can't overlook the fact that all the filth seems to stem from his firm. There's more to be uncovered there.

When the file transfer is complete, I quickly initiate the search on Maddox's print. I check the time. One minute to spare. I push away from the desk right as Rodney enters the room.

He gives me a curious look. "Tommy had to meet Emily about something," I answer his unspoken question.

He nods a few times. "Boy's whipped," he says, then proceeds toward his station.

In the center of his screen, an image flashes, highlighted in bold red. Suspect found.

"Holy shit." He taps the keyboard. "We got a hit."

Indeed. A bad parking habit put Maddox in the system. What a way for a dirty lawyer to go down.

I start to head off, then pause. I near Rodney's station, hoping to sound casual. "Oh, by the way. Could you check on a search I had Carson run?"

Rodney holds up a finger as he puts a call in to Agent Bell on the print. Tension coils my muscles tight. The inked script on my chest flashes before my eyes as if mocking me. I should sear the words from my flesh.

I've crossed my own line. I've separated myself from law and justice…and at my worst, I have become judge, jury, and executioner.

When he completes his update, Rodney digs through a number of ongoing searches and pulls up the one on A_King. The handle I gave Carson yesterday. "We didn't get anything…" He clicks through multiple screens. "Right away. This person was buried pretty damn good. But then a ping on a server in Thailand pulled up a traceable connection to Alex King."

Alex King. A. K.—the initials Avery saw embroidered on her abductor's tie. A_King—the forum user who questioned Avery about the aphrodisiac.

"Just like that?" I ask.

He ticks his head on a shrug. "I found it odd, too. This person didn't exist, then he did. When I started digging, it appeared to be an alias. This is the person behind the handle." He moves aside so I get a clear view of the screen.

The eyes I stared into last night look back at me now. Like a phantom limb, I feel the weight of my gun in my hand, my finger squeezing the trigger, as I look at the Alpha.

"Dorian McGregor," Rodney says. "Who doesn't have a rap sheet. Clean. No criminal history. But all his aliases…"

"Rap sheets longer than Santa's naughty list," I say.

Rodney laughs. "You could say that. He's one busy man on the darknet, that's for sure."

"Thanks, Rodney. I appreciate you guys looking into this."

I leave the tech department. That settles it, then. By all appearances, Dorian McGregor is the head of a crime ring operating under the guise of the Alpha Omega network. All corners match up. All angles align. It's clean, it's simple, it's a closed case.

Except for the burning suspicion in my gut.

The Feds wanted this wrapped up neat and tidy. And it is. About the time the Feds were tracing the Alpha's signal, the tech report pinging Alex King was timestamped, linking him to Dorian McGregor.

Just like the auction bust that went down without a hitch last night, the revealing evidence became available all at once on Dorian McGregor. Convenient.

Bell mentioned a protected source gave the FBI the tip on the auction—but who? Who wanted the Feds to find that warehouse? Who wanted us to trace Alex King to Dorian McGregor?

The floor beneath my feet seems to open up underneath me, and soon the sensation of falling is pulling at all corners of my mind. None of us planned anything. Our whole operation was a setup from the start.

I pick up my pace as I head toward my office. A yellow package wedged between my door stops me short, and I yank it free. I get inside my office before I unseal the top and open the folder inside.

Completed reports. For our whole team.

Carson, Sadie, me—all our reports on the events of last

night have been completed for us, typed and printed. They document our cooperation with the Feds to pursue a lead given to the FBI on a human trafficking auction in Arlington.

Son of a bitch.

The whole time, I thought I was diverting the Feds. But the bastards were redirecting me.

I move to my door window and open the blinds. Outside my office, officers and Feds work in unison. A whir of activity fills the floor. Everyone operating together to tie up the loose ends on the case.

It may look like cooperation—but it's the calm center of the storm. I feel it charging the air. An energy buzzing with warning.

Somewhere amid the organized chaos, a suspect hides.

In plain fucking sight.

I'm out of my office and barreling toward the exit, phone pressed to my ear. Waiting with my heart in my throat to hear Avery's voice.

Avery.

CHAPTER 19

AUCTION

ALPHA

*E*nemies.

Most people have at least one.

I have countless.

Enemies come in all forms. The obvious backstabber who invades your territory and deems to overthrow your empire. The smiling *friend*—the snake—who secretly strategizes your demise with the intent to acquire your empire.

Those are the most recognizable.

The ones you see coming.

Then, there are the enemies that are a little harder to spot. You're not quite sure if they're legitimate or not. Whether they intend you harm, or may indeed be an asset.

The logic is simple, however, on how to handle enemies of all shapes and sizes. Even those skeptical ones—because they're the most dangerous of all.

Eliminate them.

The turf stealer, who thought it a wise business decision to use my empire as their own springboard, is given a tip about a shipment of "merchandise" arriving at a certain location, at a certain time.

Let your enemy steal your merchandise.

Let your enemy use your connections to organize an auction. Of course, make sure that all the groundwork is laid in preparation. Prearrange the auction, scout the venue. Give him the fucking keys to the kingdom.

The backstabber was easy. Dorian took the merchandise and the venue without too much coercion. Greed always trumps caution.

The snakes... They're a little more difficult. But Lark and Gannet provided stellar resources to vet the buyers for Dorian's auction.

One judge who decided he no longer felt obligated to return my favors. One CEO who uploaded a worm to one of my accounts to filter small increments of my money into one of his banks in the Caymans. And eight other snakes that were skimming off the top of my transactions.

They've been sitting on my shit-list for a while.

In one fell swoop, the Feds provided the perfect opportunity to wipe them all out.

Of course, it wasn't all me—I'd be remiss if I didn't give credit where credit's due. The ACPD did a phenomenal job of helping to lead the Feds exactly where I wanted.

The Alpha is just a myth again. A moniker for indulgent criminal entrepreneurs to use to stake their claim in the market. The FBI Criminal Network Division appreciates the power of a name—they use it to track down leads.

And they did.

As predicted.

I stub my cigarette out in the ashtray and check the time. "Have they all arrived?"

Donovan flips on the tablet and confirms. "Twenty-six chips activated. It's a full house."

"I shouldn't keep my guests waiting, then."

Sure, I lost a large amount of revenue and a quarter of my merchandise. But some losses are expected when aiming toward long-term growth in an industry. I also vanquished a number of enemies and will soon acquire a new asset.

Doctor Avery Johnson doesn't know it yet—but she's a *very* valuable asset.

We do not halt progress; we embrace it. We keep moving forward in evolution to produce a bigger, better, superior product. Her talents shouldn't be squandered on the dead. Such a gift should be shared with the living.

Avery needs to be shown just how important she is to me.

Soon.

Very soon.

I stand at the curtain and don my mask. I step through to the stage. Larkin assumed too much; did he believe I'd ever let a narcissistic lawyer run my show?

I snap my fingers, and Donovan brings out the first of the merchandise. She's lovely. Her hair brushed to a high sheen, accentuating her natural color. Her skin polished to a rosy porcelain. No trashy bag over her head; she steps onto the stage adorned in elegant, jeweled lingerie, and draped in a sheer, flowing wrap.

She's a genie freed from her bottle. And her new Master will pay a fortune to capture her.

"Sirs, allow me to demonstrate the real reason you're here today." I lift my chin. "Can I have a volunteer?"

I have Donovan escort one of the eager men from the front row onstage. "Excellent." I prep the syringe, and the man flinches. "Don't worry. This isn't for you."

My lovely creature has been tested twice. She doesn't even fight when I place the needle to her arm. No, I rather think she enjoys it. The drug strips her of all inhibition, leaving behind the raw truth of her. The whore in her purest form.

As soon as the Trifecta hits her system, she comes to life, an animated doll. I've given her a larger dose this time so she'll wow our investors. And she does. She climbs the man on stage, pawing at his suit and tearing at her lingerie.

A wave of silent awe hushes the crowd as they watch, enraptured, as she pleads for gratification. She whines and grinds against the man until he's forced to throw her over the table and fuck her.

I wait patiently for him to get his fill. When he does,

207

zipping up his pants, she kneels before him and begs to suck his cock. "I'll take her," he says, and a light peal of laughter erupts around the room. "One million."

I smile. "Do I have any other bids?"

Hands slap down on the chair buttons, an angelic chorus to my ears.

It was an insult to think I would ever allow my girls and my Trifecta to go for anything less than a million. That should've tipped them all off that the auction was a farce. Those bottom feeders could never afford the luxury I'm offering the world.

But what do any of them know of luxury? Of dreams?

Before you can achieve your goals, you must first be daring enough to dream them.

That is the legacy of my empire.

And no one, *no one* stands in my way.

Titles by
TRISHA WOLFE

Broken Bonds Series

With Visions of Red: Broken Bonds, Book One

With Visions of Red: Broken Bonds, Book Two

With Vision of Red: Broken Bonds, Book Three

With Ties that Bind: A Broken Bonds Novel, Book One

With Ties that Bind: A Broken Bonds Novel, Book Two

With Ties that Bind: A Broken Bonds Novel, Book Three

Derision: A Novel

Living Heartwood Novels

The Darkest Part: Living Heartwood (Book 1)

Losing Track: Living Heartwood (Book 2)

Fading Out: Living Heartwood (Book 3)

Darkly, Madly Series

Born, Darkly: Darkly, Madly Duet 1

Born, Madly: Darkly, Madly Duet 2

ACKNOWLEDGMENTS

Thank you to:

My amazingly talented critique partner and friend, P.T. Michelle, for reading so quickly, giving me the much needed pep talks and advice, wonderful notes, and for your friendship.

My super human beta readers, who read on the fly and offer so much encouragement, I could not write books without your brilliance. Honestly, you are my girls! Katrina Tinnon, Naomi Hopkins, Amy Bosica, Michell Casper, and Melissa Fisher. I really can't express how much you mean to me—just know that I couldn't do this without you. Thank you.

A special shout out to the girls who keep me sane in the Wolfe Club, where it's perfectly acceptable to be anything but ;) You girls are the best. You make me laugh, keep me motivated, and offer so much support, you have no idea. I adore every single one of you. And a special thank you to my girls in the group for helping me get this book in shape! Thank you!

My awesome assistant, Naomi Hopkins. I could not get through one book without your insightful input, girl. You go above and beyond an assistant's duties to help me sort through my chaotic life. Thank you for being a friend.

To my family. My son, Blue, who is my inspiration, thank you for being you. I love you. And my husband, Daniel, for your support and owning your title as "the husband" at every book event. I love you, too. To my parents, Debbie and Al, for the emotional support, chocolate, and unconditional love—I love you guys right back.

Najla Qamber of Najla Qamber Designs, thank you for so much for not just creating this stunning, take-my-breath-away cover, but for also just rocking so hard! You were so much fun to worth with; you took the stress right out of the very stressful task of series cover creation, and I cannot wait to work with you again on future projects. This cover is everything I envisioned and more.

A special acknowledgement to Damaris, thank you for being not only a wonderful friend, who's there when I just need to call someone, but also a huge support of my career. You mean so much to me.

There are many, oh, so many people who I have to thank, who have been right beside me during this journey, and who will continue to be there, but I know I can't thank everyone here, the list would go on and on! So just know that I love you dearly. You know who you are, and I wouldn't be here without your support. Thank you so much.

To my readers, you have no idea how much I value and love each and every one of you. If it wasn't for you, none of this could be possible. As cliché as that sounds, I mean it from the bottom of my heart; I adore you, and hope to always put out books that make you laugh, swoon, and cry.

I owe everything to God, thank you for everything.

ABOUT THE AUTHOR

From an early age, Trisha Wolfe dreamed up imaginary worlds and characters and was accused of talking to herself. Today, she lives in South Carolina with her family and writes full time, using her imaginary worlds as an excuse to continue talking to herself. Get updates on future releases and events at TrishaWolfe.com

58481321R10126

Made in the USA
Middletown, DE
07 August 2019